ESCAPE WITH ME

A WITH ME IN SEATTLE NOVEL

KRISTEN PROBY

AMPERSAND PUBLISHING, INC.

Escape With Me
A With Me In Seattle Novel
By
Kristen Proby

For my tribe of friends. My ride or dies. You know who you are.

PROLOGUE

~IZZY~

*W*hat in the hell am I doing?

The pastor we booked fourteen months ago speaks, but I'm not listening. I stare up at the man I'm in the process of marrying, hoping to feel just a glimmer of the love and excitement I felt when he proposed last year on Valentine's Day. I want to feel the joy.

But his blue eyes are cold, his lips curled into a smirk, replacing the sweet smiles he once gave me— back when I fell in love with him.

He's the appropriate man. His credentials look great on paper. My *father* loves him to death. Our families have been close for as long as I can remember.

But I feel…*nothing.*

"Izzy," he whispers, squeezing my hands painfully to get my attention.

"What? Oh." I swallow and look at the pastor. "Can you please repeat that?"

"Do you take this man to be your lawfully wedded husband?"

I glance at my parents and then back up at the man before me and know in my heart of hearts what the answer is.

What it's been for a long, long time.

"No." I shake my head and pull my hands away as Troy's face scrunches up in a furious scowl. "No, this isn't what I want at all."

I turn to the audience. My father stands, his face full of confusion.

"I'm sorry. I'll call later."

And with that, I take off down the aisle and into the bridal suite so I can grab my purse and phone. Then, I hurry to my little convertible waiting outside, the one covered in balloons and a *JUST MARRIED* sign on the back.

As I pull out of the church parking lot, I see Troy walking out the door, his hands in his pockets, his mouth set.

He's not heartbroken.

He's embarrassed.

And I just dodged a proverbial bullet.

CHAPTER 1

~KEEGAN~

"*Y*ou're on my last bleeding nerve, Mary Margaret." I toss the white towel onto the bar and glare at my youngest sister.

"Back at you." She rolls her eyes as she flips her red hair over her shoulder and stomps away to the kitchen, most likely to bitch about me to our brother, Shawn, and his lovely new wife, Lexi.

Running a family business is at once satisfying and a pain in my ass.

I bought O'Callaghan's Pub from my da about five years ago when he told me that he and Ma wanted to retire and move back to Ireland. The pub is my passion, so the decision was a quick and easy one. And, I can admit, having my siblings around to help is one of the reasons I love it so much.

We're a big family. Loud and opinionated, but

loving and ready to jump in at a moment's notice if any of us needs the other.

The O'Callaghans are a tight clan, and that's the truth.

Maggie is the baby of the family and one of my best friends. She works for me full time as a waitress and a fill-in cook when the need arises.

But she's been in a foul mood all day, which isn't like her. Though when I asked what had her panties in a wad, she snarled and snapped at me like an angry badger.

I hear a dish break in the kitchen, and then Maggie stomps out of the swinging door, looking just as happy as when she went in there moments ago.

Which is to say, not happy at all.

"Maggie." I try a different tactic, calming my voice as I open my arms. "Come here, darling."

She looks as if she might flip me the bird, but then her shoulders slump, and she walks into my embrace, hugging me back.

"What's bothering you today, love?"

"Men suck."

Given that I'm her brother, and she doesn't see me as a *man*, I don't take offense.

"Man trouble, is it, then?"

"I'm being silly. And I'm sorry for calling you a horse's ass."

"You didn't."

"Well, in my head, I did." She pulls back with a

smile. "And I broke a plate in the kitchen. You can take it out of my pay."

"We'll let this one pass," I reply, relieved to see that her feathers are somewhat smoothed for now. I don't like seeing either of my sisters out of sorts. "If you need to talk, I have two ears that work just fine."

"Yeah." She sighs and then shrugs a shoulder. "There's really nothing to talk about. I'll just go splash some water on my face and get back to it. It's not even dinnertime yet. I can't let a man's lack of consideration ruin my whole day."

She saunters off to the ladies' bathroom just as the front door of my pub opens, and I feel my eyes go wide.

Having worked in this establishment all of my life, I'd thought I'd seen everything there was to see.

I was wrong.

Because right there, before my very eyes, is a princess.

There's a princess in my bar.

She walks in, looking a bit lost and worse for wear now that she's inside.

Soaking-wet from head to toe, her gown looks damn heavy. Her blond hair is saggy and coming loose from some sort of fancy up-do. Her makeup is smeared under her eyes as if she's been crying or got caught in a torrential downpour.

Given the state of the rest of her, I'd say it was the latter.

Or both.

"Come on in, lass."

She looks at me and walks to the bar, hops up onto a stool, and leans on her elbows.

"I'm getting your floor wet," she says as her phone starts lighting up in her hand.

"It'll mop up easily enough." I pour her a shot of whiskey without her asking and set it in front of her. "You look like you can use that."

Her blue eyes focus on the glass, and then she shoots it back and coughs. "That's good."

I laugh and pour her some more. "Is it raining out there?"

"Not right now," she says. "I was driving a convertible, and it rained between here and Portland."

I blink at her. "You could have pulled over and put up the top."

She nods. "Oh, I guess I could have. I didn't think of it."

"Do you need a doctor, darling?"

She shakes her head and drinks the whiskey, still ignoring the phone on the bar. "No. I don't know what I need, to be honest. I was supposed to be married by now, but I escaped that, just in the nick of time."

And here we go. It's natural for people to spill their guts to bartenders. Why, I have no idea, but they do. So, I do what I do best and start washing glasses behind the bar while the gorgeous little thing gets ready to babble away.

But to my surprise, she clenches her lips and just stares at her phone.

"Are you going to check that?"

"I should." But she doesn't reach for it. Finally, she pulls it to her and huffs out a breath. "My father just fired me."

I raise a brow. "You work for your father?"

"Not anymore," she says, then taps the screen a few times before tossing her phone into her bag. "They're pretty mad."

"Perhaps if you explain the why of it all, they won't be angry."

She watches me. "You're probably right. But for now, I do *not* want to go home. I don't want to see *him* or talk about why I left. I just want to be gone for a while. You know?"

"Like a vacation?"

"A vacation from my life," she agrees. "I don't even know how I got on this island. I drove until I came to the ferry terminal, and then I got on it—and ended up here."

"Well, it's a fine island to get lost on."

"Okay, I think I can handle whatever the day might throw at us—" Maggie stops short when she sees our customer and frowns. "Oh, honey. Are you okay? Do you need to go to the hospital?"

The other woman laughs and shakes her head. "I must really look horrible if everyone is asking me if I need medical attention."

"I think you looked better this morning," Maggie says. "Are you hungry?"

"Actually, I'm starving."

"I'll get you some stew. I'm Maggie, by the way."

"Izzy." She smiles. "I'm Izzy."

Maggie bustles to the kitchen to fetch the stew, and Izzy continues watching me.

"What's your name?" she asks.

"Keegan O'Callaghan."

"You're a handsome one," she says, then her eyes go wide. "And that's the whiskey talking. But it's true. But I'm off all men, so you're safe from me. No need to throw me out or anything."

I laugh and decide not to give her any more whiskey.

"I'm not throwing you out of here."

"Good."

Maggie returns with the stew, and Izzy digs in. "This is delicious."

"Thanks." Maggie smiles. "It's a family recipe."

"Our ma used to be in charge of the kitchen here at O'Callaghan's," I say.

"You two are siblings?" she asks.

"That's right," Maggie says. "And three others come in and out from time to time. Shawn and his wife are manning the kitchen today."

"Where are the other two?" Izzy asks, seeming enthralled by the story.

"Kane is probably working on something in his barn," I reply, "and Maeve is likely showing houses."

"So, you all live around here?"

"Aye. Where are you from, Izzy?"

"Salem, just south of Portland." She sighs. "And I'm not going back for a while."

"What are you going to do?" Maggie asks.

"I don't know."

I've never been able to turn away someone in need. "I can use another waitress."

Izzy's eyes light up. "Really? Can I apply for the job? I know I'm not exactly dressed for an interview, but I'm a hard worker."

"Have you waitressed before?"

Her expression falls. "No. But I learn fast, and I'm totally trustworthy. And I could really use the job."

Maggie walks behind Izzy then gives me a grin and a thumbs-up. She wants me to hire her.

"Can you start this evening?"

"I can start right now." She looks down at herself. "Wait. I don't even have any clothes. I left the church so fast, I didn't take anything but my purse with me."

"I have some things you can borrow," Maggie offers. "Keegan, I'd like to take her home so she can shower and get into something much more comfortable."

"I can handle things here for a while."

"Does that mean I can start tonight?" Izzy asks.

"I do believe you just got yourself a job," I reply.

Izzy claps her hands and hops off her stool. "Thank you. So much. You won't regret it."

SIX HOURS LATER, I already regret it.

Not having Izzy around. With all the makeup cleaned off her face, and after a shower and some clean clothes, she's absolutely gorgeous. And she's kind, funny, and good with the customers.

But she's a horrible waitress.

Izzy hurries to the bar with her tray, stops and blinks, and then turns back and yells at the table across the room. "What kind of beer did you say you wanted, Frank?"

I sigh. "Know the customers' names, do you?"

"They're super nice," she says.

They think she's hot. That's why they're so fucking nice.

"But you can't remember their orders?"

She bites her lip. "I know, I'm sorry."

I slide a pad of paper and a pen across the bar to her. "Write the orders down. You don't have to remember them."

"Maggie doesn't write anything down."

"Maggie's been working in this pub since she was in nappies, Izzy. Trust me, just write it all down."

She takes the pad and smiles shyly. I've noticed that she keeps looking at our small stage, watching the duo who plays Irish music for us on the weekends.

"They're good."

"They are, yes."

Without another word, she goes back to Frank's table and writes down their order. The rest of the evening is busy. I can see that Izzy's feet hurt, but she doesn't complain. She doesn't mess up another order, only breaks one glass, and is true to her word.

She learns quickly.

At the end of the night, once the door is locked and the bar cleaned up, I catch Izzy yawning with a mop in her hand.

"I think that's enough excitement for you today."

"I can finish," she insists.

"We're done," Maggie announces.

"Oh, thank God," Izzy says with a small laugh. "I'm so dang tired. I was supposed to be in Aruba right now. Instead, I'm here. I'm not complaining. I just—"

"I totally get it," Maggie assures her.

"You did well," I say as I turn off the lights and get ready to follow the girls out to their cars. We've never had a problem here, but it's the middle of the night, and I'd rather make sure they're safe.

"Thank you so much. I had fun. When is my next shift?"

"Tomorrow afternoon," I reply. "Be here around noon. You can work until dinnertime."

"Awesome."

"Goodnight," Maggie says with a wave and gets into her car.

I watch as Izzy climbs into her little Lexus convertible. But instead of starting it up and driving away, she reclines the driver's seat and locks the doors.

I drag my hand down my face.

You have *got* to be kidding me.

I prop my hands on my hips and look around. It's none of my business if Izzy wants to sleep in her car.

She's a grown woman.

This is a safe town.

I turn around to walk back inside, then mumble *fuck* under my breath and approach Izzy's car.

I tap on the window, startling her.

She turns the key and lowers the glass.

"Am I not allowed to park here?"

"Parking here isn't the issue. You don't have anywhere to go?"

She shakes her head. "But I'm fine here. It's warm. Maggie loaned me a blanket, so it'll be fine."

I try to open the door, but it's locked. "Come with me."

"Where?"

"Inside. You can sleep in my flat until you get your feet under you."

"Oh, that's not necessary. I don't want to impose. You've already done so much for me—"

"Izzy. I'm not going to let you sleep out here in your

car when I have space for you upstairs. Now, get your things and come with me."

She blows out a breath, then does as I ask. She locks her car behind her as she follows me into the bar and up the steps to the flat above.

"Wait, you're not a serial killer, right?"

"Now's not the smartest time to remember to ask me that."

"But, for real, though."

"No, I'm not going to hurt you. Come on."

I open the door, relieved that I took an extra twenty minutes this morning to straighten things up.

"It's not big, but it's home."

There's a tiny kitchenette off the living room. I show her the master—and only—bedroom, then lead her to the bathroom.

"I have all the essentials in here. I'll set out a new toothbrush and razor for you."

"Wow, thank you so much, Keegan."

And just like it was all night, it's like a punch to the fucking gut when she says my name.

"You're welcome. I'll change the sheets on the bed for you."

"I'm definitely not taking your bed. I can sleep just fine on the couch."

"My ma would have my hide if she knew I let you sleep on the sofa." I smile at her and turn to the linen closet for fresh sheets. Less than ten minutes later, my bedroom belongs to Izzy, and I have a blanket and a pillow waiting for me in the living room. "Just let me know if you need anything."

I walk into the kitchen to make myself a cup of tea and hear Izzy walking into the bathroom. The shower starts. I lean on the countertop, my head hanging, chin touching my chest.

The sexiest woman I've ever seen in my life is naked in my shower, about to sleep in my flat, and she's totally off-limits.

She's only hours from running out of her wedding.

And she works for me.

But, damn it, something about her pulls at me.

The water turns off, and I can picture her drying herself with a fluffy, white towel. The bathroom door opens. She shuts off the light and shuffles back to the bedroom, wearing a pair of Maggie's sweats and an old college T-shirt.

I carry my tea to the sofa and let it steep on the coffee table as I take the fastest shower of my life, given the lack of hot water. I pull on some clean clothes and return to the living room to lie down. My feet hang over the end of the armrest. My shoulders are too wide for the cushions.

I'm a damn giant on this thing.

I shift onto my side and watch the steam rising from my mug.

The light under the bedroom door goes out, and the flat becomes still in the night.

What the fuck am I doing?

CHAPTER 2

I hear rain.

Does it rain this hard in Aruba?

I stretch under the covers and frown at the soreness in my ankles and feet. I open my eyes and frown.

I'm not in Aruba.

I'm in Washington.

In a strange man's bed.

Alone.

Yesterday's events roll through my mind, from running out on the wedding to the long drive, and Keegan giving me a job. I should feel guilty. Sad. But I don't. All I feel is relief.

I sit up and reach for my phone, turning it on. I'm sure I have dozens of messages waiting for me. After my dad sent me the pleasant message that I'd embarrassed the family, hurt his friends, and was fired and on my own, I'd turned off the phone and didn't give it another thought for the rest of the day.

I yawn and rub my hands over my face as the screen comes to life, and then frown when I see I only have *one* missed text.

From Troy.

Where do you want me to send your shit?

That's it. No worried messages from my friends or my mom. Just Troy wondering where to ship the few things I have at his house.

I do a quick Google search for O'Callaghan's Pub, then copy and paste the address and hit send.

"Well, that's pathetic," I mutter as I get out of bed and open the bedroom door. I need the restroom and food, in that order.

When I walk toward the kitchen, I glance over and see Keegan asleep on the small couch in the living room. He looks massive on the tiny sofa. He's lying on his back, his feet propped on the armrest, his arms crossed over his chest.

His very bare chest.

I guess standing and ogling another man less than twenty-four hours after fleeing the altar is a strong indicator that my marriage to Troy wasn't a good idea.

But Keegan is long and lean, tanned and muscled—his abs are what a girl's dreams are made of. And even in sleep, he has the slightest little scowl line between his eyebrows.

Keegan doesn't strike me as a grumpy man, but he has that sexy crease.

"Are you just going to stand there and stare at me, then?" he says without opening his eyes.

I feel my cheeks flush. "I thought you were asleep."

He rubs his hands over his face and then sits up on the side of the sofa. "I was until I felt someone staring at me."

"Sorry." I shuffle my feet. "Want me to make some coffee?"

"No, I think we should both get dressed, and I'll take you out for breakfast at my favorite place."

"Oh, you don't have to—"

"I'm going with or without you," he says but softens his tone with a small smile. "It's my daily routine. And you're welcome to join me."

My stomach growls, and I nod. "Thanks. I'd like that."

It doesn't take long for me to get dressed and ready to go—hair tied back in a ponytail, a bit of mascara and lip gloss I had stowed in my purse applied. I'm beyond lucky that Maggie and I are roughly the same size and that she has such an extensive closet. I borrowed several days' worth of clothes to get me through until I make enough money to buy some things for myself.

When Keegan's ready, we set out down a flight of stairs behind the pub that leads to his truck waiting in the alley.

With a turn of the key, Keegan's Toyota 4x4 roars to

life, and he pulls out of the parking space and onto the main road.

"So, you go out to breakfast every morning?" I ask, trying to make conversation.

"Most days. I don't cook, and I like this diner. Good people own it."

I'm watching the town pass by as we make our way through the heart of it. "It's such a *cute* town. I didn't pay much attention yesterday."

"You had other things on your mind," he says. "We're a small community of just over three-thousand people. We swell to twice that size in tourist season, but given we're nearing the end of summer, things are about to slow down."

"I bet that's not good for your business."

"It's true that summer is the best time for the pub, but I stay busy enough all year through. We have our steady regulars, who want to come by for a pint or just some conversation. And the music brings in a good crowd on the weekends. My parents established roots in this community, and they're sturdy ones."

"I could tell last night that a lot of the customers were regulars," I reply. "I like your pub very much, Keegan."

He smiles, and I swear it could light up all of the Pacific Northwest. "Thank you, lass."

Lass. Jesus God Almighty, that accent is ridiculously sexy. I've never been a woman to swoon over a foreign accent. Maybe it's because I've spent a lot of time abroad with my family, and it just never did anything for me.

But Keegan's accent is smooth and lyrical. Like the gorgeous music played in his pub.

He parks on the street in front of a retro-looking diner on the corner. It appears as if it's been here since the town began.

When we walk inside, everyone looks up and waves at Keegan. It's very much like the show *Cheers*, and it makes me laugh.

"So, you know everyone, then."

He nods as we sit in a booth. "Small town, Izzy."

"What's good?" I ask as I look at the menu before me. "Is there a local favorite here?"

"The cinnamon rolls are a religious experience," he says.

"You don't have a menu."

"No. I get the same thing every day."

"And what is that?"

"Oatmeal with raisins and a side of toast."

"You come all the way across town for oatmeal?"

"And coffee."

I grin at him just as the waitress walks over to us. "Your usual today, Keegan?"

"Yes, please. And whatever Izzy's having, of course."

"I want two eggs, scrambled, some hash browns, and bacon. And a cinnamon roll."

The waitress raises a brow. "You must be hungry."

"I am."

19

She fills both our cups with coffee and then wanders off to place our orders.

"How do you feel today?" Keegan asks.

"My feet are a little sore," I confess. "I'm just not used to working on them, but I'll adjust."

"And how about mentally?"

I stir the creamer into my coffee, then take a sip and frown at him over the rim of the cup. "What do you mean?"

"You walked out on a wedding yesterday. I'm curious as to how you feel about it today."

"Oh." I take another sip and feel the caffeine start to flow through my veins. "Well, Troy texted me this morning and asked where he should send my *shit*, as he called it. So, I gave him the pub's address. I hope that's okay."

"It's fine." He sips his black coffee. "And doesn't answer my question."

"I'm relieved. And I'm happy to be here. That's all I know for now."

"It's a good start."

I don't want to confess that no one cares where I am today. That the only message waiting for me this morning was from my ex-fiancé, and he wasn't at all concerned, just wanted to know where to send my stuff.

I've had crappy people in my life for a *long* time, and it's only more glaringly obvious today. I don't want to admit that to Keegan.

It's embarrassing.

"Holy crap," I say as the waitress returns with our meals. She's carrying a huge tray on her shoulder, and I practically swallow my tongue when I see the size of the cinnamon roll. "This is huge."

"Don't worry, we can box up anything you can't put away here," the waitress says with a wink and then walks away.

"You're going to help me eat this," I inform Keegan, who just grins at me from across the table.

"That's what I was counting on."

"I CAN'T BELIEVE these words are about to come out of my mouth." I've just buckled my seatbelt after the most delicious breakfast of my life, and I am pretty sure I gained fifteen pounds.

So worth it.

"But I have to stop at the store, or a Target, some-place for some essentials and snacks."

"Snacks?" Keegan pulls out into light traffic.

"Yes. I'm a snacker. I can't help it. Is there a Target in town?"

"Sure." He doesn't have to drive far before he's pulling into the parking lot.

"This shouldn't take long."

"No hurry."

Once inside, I make a beeline for the shampoo

section. I don't have much money since Dad cut me off, but I have some cash from last night's tips, and I need a few things. I grab some shampoo and conditioner—not my usual expensive brand, but it will do. I also snag some deodorant before wandering over to the snacks.

I grin when I see that the Goldfish are on sale and toss a bag into my basket.

"Don't judge me," I warn Keegan as I grab some graham crackers. "I'm a seven-year-old when it comes to snacks."

He just laughs, but when we make our way to the pizza Lunchables, and I reach for one, he shakes his head.

"This one, I'll judge you for. If you want pizza, we'll buy pizza."

"Pizza is my favorite."

"What you have in your hand isn't real pizza."

"Fine." I sigh and put it back, then smile when I see my favorite wine on an end cap. I reach for a bottle and hear Keegan sigh next to me. "What?"

"You know I own a bar, right? There's no need to buy the wine."

"Do you serve this brand? Because it's my favorite."

"I guess I do now," he mutters and takes a picture of the bottle with his phone.

"Okay, this will do for today."

He nods and leads me to the checkout. After the cashier rings up my things, he reaches for his wallet, and I shake my head.

"This is my junk, Keegan."

"You don't have any money."

"Yes, I do. I have tips from last night." I pass the cash over to the cashier and accept my bags from her. When we're outside, I glance up at him. "I appreciate you wanting to help. I really do. But you've already gone above and beyond. I can pay for my own shampoo and Goldfish."

"Understood."

"You're done for the day," Keegan says at around seven in the evening. "You can grab some dinner here, if you like."

"I've been eyeing more of that stew all day," I say as I untie my apron. "I feel like such an idiot."

"Because you like stew?"

"No." I lean on the bar and smile at him. "Because this is just so *hard.* I feel so clumsy and slow. Maggie breezes around here like some kind of Irish faerie, taking orders and making people smile. She even *sang* earlier while she delivered drinks. And I can barely carry the tray with a food order without making a fool of myself."

"You're being too hard on yourself, lass," he says. "Now, go get yourself a bowl of stew and come have a seat."

I nod and walk through the swinging door to where

Keegan's brother, Shawn, mans the kitchen. His wife, Lexi, fills a basket full of fries.

"Whenever you have a moment, I'd love a bowl of stew," I say when Lexi looks over with a smile.

"Of course." She reaches for a bowl to ladle a scoop into and then adds a crusty piece of bread to the side. "How was your shift today, Izzy?"

"Oh, just fine, thanks. I'm going to take this to the bar."

Lexi nods and then gets back to filling orders with Shawn.

I've just taken a bite of my stew when Keegan approaches and sets a glass of wine on the bar for me. I take a sip and then stare at him in surprise.

"This is the wine I showed you today."

"It is, yes."

"You didn't have to go back out and get it."

"It's not a big deal." He wipes the bar with his white towel. "You look knackered."

"If that means exhausted, you'd be right. Maybe the past couple of days finally caught up with me."

He nods and watches as I eat my dinner. "Well, go on up when you've finished here and make yourself at home."

"Thank you. Really, Keegan."

"You're welcome."

And with that, he wanders away to fill drink orders and chat with the customers. Keegan is an attentive bartender. His patrons enjoy sitting at the bar rather than the high-top tables so they can sit and chat with him as they drink a pint of beer or eat their dinner.

Keegan's a good listener and knows when to refill a glass or cut someone off who's had a bit too much. He reads the room well, and he's quick with a laugh, or even to join Maggie for a song—which surprised me.

He has a wonderful singing voice.

It's been fun watching Keegan, Maggie, and Shawn together. Their love for each other is evident. I didn't realize that families got along like this outside of fiction.

Once I've finished my dinner, I take my dishes to the kitchen and then climb the stairs to Keegan's apartment above. Finally, with no eyes on me, I can move a bit slower.

My feet are screaming. The blisters are bad enough, but add in my sore ankles and achy toes, and I want to cry.

Still, I make it upstairs and flop down on the couch. I turn on the TV to have some noise and lean my head back against the cushions.

I must fall asleep because the next thing I know, Keegan is standing over me and shutting off the TV.

"Oh, sorry. I fell asleep."

His lips twitch as I stand, and then he scowls when I turn to walk away.

"Why are you limping?"

"My feet are just a little sore."

"Sit." His stern voice leaves no room for argument.

I do as he asks, and he kneels in front of me and unties the shoes Maggie lent me. When he peels off the socks, he gasps.

"My God, you're fucking bleeding, Izzy."

"Yeah, the blisters are a bitch. And my ankles are sore."

"You needn't have worked your feet into bloody stumps."

"I'm fine," I insist, but he stands and stomps into the bathroom. I hear the tub filling, and then he returns and lifts me right off the couch. "I can walk, you know."

"Not on these feet, you can't." He sits me on a stool next to the tub, and when it's the temperature he likes, he urges me to put my feet in. "It's going to sting on those blisters for a second, but you need to soak your feet, lass."

Honestly, as long as he calls me *lass*, I'll do whatever he wants.

He's right. The blisters sting when they hit the warm water, but after a few moments, it subsides. Keegan disappears for a bit, but when he returns, he has a hot cup of tea.

"I added honey because you like your drinks sweet."

"How do you know that?"

"The wine you like is sweet, and you added sugar to your coffee this morning."

I eye him as I sip the tea. "It's delicious, thank you."

He kneels next to the tub and reaches in to see to

my feet. It's quite nice to simply sip a hot drink while someone washes my feet in a warm tub.

He drains the water, then gently pats my skin dry. Once again, he lifts me to take me to the bedroom.

"You can change." He takes the teacup out of my hand. "I'll be right back."

I blink at him. He's being *so nice* to me.

I quickly change back into Maggie's sweats and T-shirt just as Keegan knocks on the door and comes in carrying another cup of hot tea and a bottle of lotion.

"Go ahead and get comfortable," he says.

"You really don't have to do this."

"I'm the reason your feet hurt like this."

"I'm pretty sure it's because I'm wearing shoes half a size too big." But I do as he asks and get comfortable on the bed. He's careful not to rub the lotion over the blisters as he massages it into my skin. His hands are so *strong.* When he digs his thumb into the arch of my foot, I have to bite my lip so I don't moan in delight.

I lean back and close my eyes.

"If you keep rubbing my feet, I'm going to fall asleep," I warn him.

"That's not a bad thing," he murmurs, not stopping at my warning. His hands feel good on my skin, and with the warm tea in my belly, I relax and feel all the stress of the day melt away.

I take a deep breath and let it out slowly.

"If the whole bar ownership thing doesn't work out for you, you could go to massage school."

I open my eyes, expecting to see him with that sexy smirk on his lips, but his gaze is intent on my face.

"Keegan?"

He shakes his head as if pulling himself out of a trance. "You should be good now. Sleep well."

And with that, he leaves the room and gently closes the door behind him.

Was it something I said?

CHAPTER 3

~IZZY~

*I*t's been a whole two weeks since I left my life and everything I knew. My feet are healed, with the help of shoes that fit—thanks to several nights' worth of tips. It also didn't hurt that Keegan insisted I take a day off to rest them and fronted me one day of sick time.

I don't know how I stumbled across such a generous group of people, but I'm so grateful. Some-day, I *will* pay it forward.

"These are the last of the empties from my tables," I inform Keegan as I set the heavy tray on the bar. "I can wash them if you'd like."

"No, you've had a full day." He flashes me a smile that makes my toes curl in my new sneakers. Another something that's happened in the past two weeks…my attraction to my boss has grown by leaps and bounds.

But I'm a professional, and not one to try to seduce the hand that feeds her.

I'm not stupid.

Not to mention, he's never given me any indication that he's being anything but nice to me.

He pours me a glass of wine and offers it to me with a wink. "Why don't you take this upstairs and unwind, Izzy?"

"I will *not* turn down that offer." I accept the wine and turn to head upstairs to the apartment. I climb the steps and take a sip of the sweet wine that Keegan always has on hand now.

I feel a little guilty that he still won't let me sleep on the couch. I know it has to be uncomfortable for him sleeping on that thing, but he won't even entertain the idea of trading with me. I've looked for a small apartment, but I haven't been working here long enough to afford first, last, and a deposit.

And there's no way I'll ask my father for help—not that he'd give it, even if I *did* ask.

I change out of my dirty T-shirt and jeans into black yoga pants and an oversized sweater that hangs off one shoulder 80s-style, then sit on the couch with my glass of wine when a text comes through from a friend back home.

This is the first time she—or any of my *friends*—has reached out to me since the wedding. And, yes, I understand that it only reiterates that I have some shitty people in my life.

I open my phone.

Mindy: *OMG! Did you see this??*

She included a screenshot of Troy's Instagram page. I unfollowed the page last week, but now I open the app and search for his name. Troy has a public profile, so I don't have an issue with seeing the images.

Photo after photo of my ex-fiancé in Aruba—on *my honeymoon*—with none other than Heather Croy. My supposed friend. Ex-friend now, the way she's hanging all over him.

I don't bother replying to Mindy. She's only stirring shit. Doing a good job of it, obviously, but I don't want to give her the satisfaction of a response.

I stand and pace the living room. I can hear the music downstairs as I drink wine and look at the photos over and over again.

He went on my vacation.

He took *my* friend.

I wonder if they were sleeping together before the wedding. Looking back now, it honestly wouldn't surprise me if Troy had been cheating on me for a long time.

I finish my wine and frown. I'm going to need much more of this.

I march out the door and down the stairs to the bar. Keegan's eyebrow raises when he takes me in and then he cocks his head to the side. "Problem, sweetheart?"

"I want to get drunk." I hop up onto a stool. "Take the tab out of my paycheck."

His eyes narrow. "All right then, if it's drunk you want to be, I can help with that easily enough. Wine?"

"Whiskey."

He sighs and leans on the bar. "Izzy, what's bothering you?"

"None of your business." If I talk about it, I'll cry, and I'll be damned if I waste even a single tear on that asshole Troy. "I just want to drink."

"Okay, then." He pulls out a highball glass, not a shot glass this time, and pours me a good helping of Irish whiskey.

"Whoa, be careful there, lass," the man next to me says when I take a big gulp. "That whiskey is for sipping. It'll go down smooth as silk."

"What's your name?" I ask the older gentleman.

"Sam."

"Well, Sam, thank you for your advice. Are you married?"

"For nearly forty-six years now."

I grin and pat Sam's shoulder. "That's sweet. Do you still like her?"

"Do I like her?"

"Yes."

"Well, I guess there was a day or two in those years that the liking might have been in question. But the love has only grown every day."

I nod and feel warmth spreading in my chest. Whether it's the sweet words from Sam or the whiskey, I'm not entirely sure.

"That's nice. I'm glad for you, Sam." I set my glass closer to Keegan and nod at him. "More, please."

Keegan's lips press into a line as he pours me some more, but he doesn't ask again what's wrong.

I take a big sip, then decide to slow it down a bit so I don't fall on my face in the next six minutes. My lips tingle, and my head is blissfully cloudy as the band returns from their break and begins a slow, sad Irish song.

Maggie bustles by and offers me a smile. "Hello there. I thought you'd left for the evening."

"I did, too, but it seems I need to get drunk."

Her eyes narrow, much like her older brother's. "Well, we all have those nights, don't we? Let me know if you need anything. Like food to sop up some of that Jameson."

"Then I wouldn't be as drunk, and that would be sad."

She chuckles and loads her tray with the drinks Keegan placed out for her. "That's true. I'll be back."

She bustles away, and I take another swig of whiskey, then blow out a breath as the liquid burns its way down my throat.

It only takes me about half an hour to get good and thoroughly buzzed. I certainly wouldn't be able to drive at this point.

There are two of everybody.

It's delightful.

"More, please," I say to Keegan, but he just slides a glass of water in front of me. "Hey, what's the big idea?"

"You need some water in you before I give you more alcohol," he says. I begrudgingly take a sip of water and frown at him over the rim. "Would you like to tell me what's got you so riled up, darling?"

"Fine." I wake up my phone and bring up the photos, then toss the cell over to Keegan.

"What am I looking at?"

"My ex with my so-called *friend* in Aruba."

His green gaze—the greenest eyes I've ever seen in my life—flies to mine.

"I don't even know why I'm upset," I admit and prop my chin in my hand. "I mean, I want nothing to do with Troy. He's a first-class jerk. And, obviously, Heather isn't my friend. But she was *in* my wedding—even though it didn't happen. And now she's all cozied up on *my* vacation. What should have been my honeymoon."

"Of course, you're upset," he says as he sets my phone down on the bar. "Even if you don't love him, it's still a betrayal."

"Mostly, I'm upset about Aruba," I admit quietly. "I was *so* excited for that vacation. I'd been working for my dad pretty much non-stop for two years, and I needed to get away. Somewhere warm and tropical."

"How long did you work for your da?"

"Since college. I wanted to be a weather girl, but my parents would *not* let me do that, even though I have a degree in meteorology and everything. They made me work for the family business, running numbers all day. And, yes, they're wealthy, and I had an indulged life living in their guest house, but everyone needs a vacation now and then. Right, Sam?"

The older man smiles my way and nods his gray head. "That they do, lass."

"I love that the Irish call me *lass*," I say with a happy sigh. "Anyway, I sound spoiled. And maybe I am. Or was. But I'm *so* happy to be out of there. I love this job way more than I did being a bookkeeper. And I hated living in the guest house. Even though I could technically come and go as I pleased, they still kept tabs on me. I'm twenty-eight years old, and my mother would always comment if I brought shopping bags home or if I got in late. And I just realized, aside from a few personal things, I don't own anything. I don't even have a couch. Or a bed."

I lay my face on my arms in despair.

"I'm pathetic."

"I don't think you're pathetic at all, sweet girl."

I raise my head at the new voice. A nice woman just down the bar smiles at me. "It sounds to me like you got yourself out of a bad situation, and that's not pathetic in my book."

"I agree," Frank, the regular customer I've been waiting on every day for two weeks, agrees from beside her.

"I love you guys," I say. "I really do. You're here for me, and that's what friends do. *You're* my real friends."

"That's right," Sam says and pats my hand in a fatherly manner, making me all warm inside.

"Maybe it's time for you to go to bed," Maggie suggests.

"Yeah." But I don't get up. "But I like hanging out with you guys. It makes me feel less alone."

"What have you done to her?" Shawn asks as he walks out of the kitchen and sees me sitting at the bar.

"Hey. Have I told you that your family is like, *hot*? Because you are. All of you. I mean, I haven't met Maeve or Kane yet, but I'm quite sure they're as good-looking as the rest of you. It should be illegal. Or at least come with a warning. You could put one of those chalkboards out front that says: *Warning - the people who work here will melt your panties right off.*"

I sip my water and look around as everyone stares at me in surprise and then busts up laughing.

"I'm not trying to be funny."

"And that's why you are," Frank says. "And you're right. The O'Callaghans are a bonny bunch, and that's the truth of it."

"Man, you aren't kidding."

Shawn kisses me on the cheek and wraps his arm around my shoulders. "How can I help you, sweet girl? Can I get you some stew?"

"Nachos," I reply. "I think this is a job for nachos."

"Coming right up."

"Hey, guys," I hear and turn at the sound of the new voice. A gorgeous blonde approaches the bar, a slightly older version of Keegan behind her. "We decided to come in for a while."

"You're the prettiest girl I've ever seen." My words are a tiny bit slurred, but I can't help myself. She *is* the prettiest girl I've ever seen.

"And you're my new best friend," she replies with a laugh.

"Stasia, this is Izzy," Keegan says. "My newest employee. Anastasia is married to my brother, Kane. The bozo behind her."

"It's nice to meet you," I say and then look down. "Oh, wow. You're pregnant. In a bar."

"I'm very pregnant," she agrees and pats her belly. "This little one should be coming along in a few weeks. Oh, and it's kicking."

"Can I feel?" I ask. "It's okay if you'd rather not, but I've never felt that before."

"Of course." She takes my hand and places it over the side of her stomach, and after just a couple of seconds, I feel a flutter under my hand.

"Oh, wow."

"The little stinker kicks me all the damn time."

"Do you know if it's a boy or a girl?" I ask.

"No." Anastasia looks up at her husband. "Kane didn't want to know until he or she is born."

"The surprise is fun," I say, feeling myself starting to

sober up. Shawn comes out of the kitchen with my nachos, Lexi on his heels.

"You're here!" Lexi exclaims and hugs Anastasia tightly. "I'm so happy you're home."

"They've been in Ireland for the past month or so," Keegan informs me.

"We're happy to be home, as well," Anastasia says. "I was worried they wouldn't let me fly because I'm so far along in my pregnancy, but I've been perfectly healthy, and the doctor gave me the thumbs-up."

"When are Ma and Da coming?" Shawn asks.

"Next week," Keegan answers. "I spoke with Da this morning."

"They wouldn't miss the birth of their first grandchild," Lexi interjects. "We're all thrilled for you."

"Even I am, and I just met you," I say as I finally take my hand away from the round belly. "That's not awkward at all."

"Nope. Because you're my new bestie, remember?" Stasia says with a wink.

Man, I really like these people.

THE NACHOS WERE A BAD IDEA.

I moan and turn over in bed, frowning when I hear what sounds like loud whispering on the other side of the bedroom door.

"You knew she was staying here." That's Keegan.

"But I *didn't* know she was sleeping in your bed," Maggie's voice retorts. "You're not supposed to sleep with the employees, Keegan, no matter how pretty they are."

Aww. She thinks I'm pretty.

"I'm *not* sleeping with her," he says. "Jesus, Mary Margaret, she's in my bed, but I sleep on the couch."

I sit up and press a hand to my head. Ugh, last night was fun, but I won't be repeating it anytime soon.

I stand and open the door, then smile at the three people on the other side.

"Hi."

Maggie turns. "Oh, good morning. We were whispering so we wouldn't wake you up."

"Right. Scream-whispering is super quiet."

The other woman laughs and then turns to Keegan. "I like her."

"You must be Maeve."

"And you're Izzy." Maeve shakes my hand. "I've heard a lot about you. I'm sorry I haven't been around. I had a conference in Hawaii and decided to stay for a couple of weeks for vacation."

I blink at her and then laugh. It's that or cry. "Seems everyone is getting tropical vacations these days."

"I highly recommend it," Maeve says and then gets an elbow to the stomach from Maggie. "What?"

"Anyway, I just wanted to save Keegan's reputation. He's not sleeping with me. He's taking the couch, which I've told him repeatedly he doesn't have to do. I would probably fit there better than he does."

"I thought there was an air mattress up here," Maggie says. "I'm so sorry, Izzy. You can come stay with me. I actually have an extra bedroom *with* a bathroom. It's just sitting there unused."

I frown and glance up at Keegan, who still hasn't said anything. "But would you be okay here by yourself?"

His lips turn up in humor as Maeve laughs her butt off.

"He's going to be just fine," Maeve insists.

"You don't have to go if you'd rather not," Keegan says. "I'm not kicking you out. But, yes, I'll be fine if you decide to go and stay with Maggie. I'll still see you when you come to work."

I nod, thinking it over. It would be nice to have a little more space, and Keegan would get his bed back.

"I think it's kind of a no-brainer. You need your bed, Keegan."

He shrugs a shoulder. "It's up to you."

"Are you sure? I can start paying you rent next month," I say to Maggie.

"Oh, we'll figure it out. And, yes, I'm sure. We can move you over this morning."

I smile, starting to get excited at the thought of sharing a place with Maggie. I've come to think of the other woman as a good friend.

"Thank you so much."

"Oh, and these arrived for you," Keegan says, pointing at two brown boxes. "I'll make you some coffee."

"Thanks." I stare at the boxes and then sigh. "Does someone have a knife?"

"Here." Keegan returns with a pocketknife, slices open the tape on the boxes, and then goes back to brewing the coffee.

The man is handy to have around.

I open the first box and find my laptop, some papers, my phone charger, makeup, and hair supplies all thrown inside.

Nothing is wrapped.

At first glance, I'd wager that my laptop is ruined.

"Dude, that's a big mess," Maeve says.

"Your poor computer," Maggie agrees.

"I guess he was a little bitter," I reply with a sigh and set the box aside, then reach for the other, bigger box. "This should be clothes."

I'm not wrong. He tossed my clothes into the box, along with a couple of pairs of shoes. One of the flats doesn't have its match. And then I scowl at a pair of pink, lace panties.

"These aren't mine."

The girls stare at me. Even Keegan turns around in surprise.

"What the fuck?" he asks.

"Exactly. You know what? Throw it all away. I don't

41

want any of it. There's nothing in there that I can't live without."

"I'll take care of it," Keegan says as he passes me a fresh mug of coffee. "And I'll hit that computer with a sledgehammer a few times, just to make sure no one can get any info off it."

"Oh, can I do that part? Might be good therapy."

CHAPTER 4

~IZZY~

"*I* shouldn't be here," I whisper to Maggie, who's standing beside me at the cake table.

"Why?" she asks. "You were invited."

"Yeah, but it's a family thing. I haven't even been around for a month yet. I definitely shouldn't be at Anastasia's baby shower."

"You and me both," Shawn says as he joins us. "Since when are men invited to these things?"

"Baby shower parties have been co-ed for a while now," Maggie informs her brother. "And it's fun."

"At least we get cake," Shawn replies.

Out of all of the siblings, Shawn is more even-keeled and the quietest. I feel like he's the calm in the storm. That the other siblings are more outspoken, the girls are certainly lively, and Shawn is this stoic, handsome guy who anchors them all.

Getting closer to the O'Callaghan family has been educational, to say the least.

"Don't overthink it," Maggie suggests to me. "It's just a fun party. A chance to eat too much, laugh a little bit, and look at cute baby things."

"I just heard from Maeve," Keegan says as he joins us. "She and the parents are on their way over."

"They must be jet lagged," I reply. "They just arrived from Ireland last night."

"Oh, I'm sure that's the truth," Keegan agrees, "but they're anxious to see everyone. Nothing could keep them away from the pub today."

I glance around and sigh in happiness. Maggie, Lexi, and I spent the morning decorating for the occasion. Pink and blue balloons, streamers, and confetti are everywhere. One table has gifts, another cake, and one more is set up for a buffet-style lunch that Lexi and Shawn have been working on for several days.

"I thought you said it would just be family," I say to Maeve.

"That's right."

"Then why so much cake? So much food? This feels excessive."

Maeve's face splits into a wide smile. "Just wait until you see Anastasia's side of the family, my friend. There's a lot of them. Also, most of them are famous."

"Famous?"

"Oh, yeah."

"More famous than Kane?" The eldest O'Callaghan sibling is a world-renowned glass sculptor.

"Somewhat, yes," she says. "You'll see."

I glance down at what I'm wearing and thank the heavens above that Maggie and I went shopping last week after my drunken debacle and the ruined boxes arriving from Troy. With my shiny new paycheck, I was able to replace the majority of my wardrobe.

I'm in a pair of black jeans with a white button-down shirt and a thick belt to tie it all together. I finally feel like myself in clothes that fit my style and make me feel more confident.

I even took the time to put on my usual makeup and teased some loose curls into my long, blond hair.

I wear my hair up in a ponytail or bun almost every day for work, so this feels extra indulgent today.

I guess I'll pass muster for famous people.

Keegan's parents arrive first, and it's a flurry of hugs and laughter and love. I step back out of the way, but Keegan's father's gaze catches mine, and he walks right over to me.

"You must be the lovely Izzy that I've heard so much about. I'm Tom O'Callaghan. How are you getting along, then?"

I smile at the thick accent and the kind face so much like his three sons. "I'm doing very well, thank you. You have incredibly kind children."

"And that's the truth of it, but it's always nice to

hear that they behave when their sainted mother and I are away."

I laugh, immediately feeling at ease with this older man. His wife joins us, and I am swept up in a firm hug. Stronger than expected from such a small woman.

"This gorgeous vision is my wife, Fiona."

"It's a pleasure to meet you."

"Well, you're even lovelier than I thought you'd be. Isn't she just a sight, Tom?"

"That she is, my love."

"Thank you. It's nice of Maggie to say such nice things, but—"

"Oh, t'wasn't Mary Margaret," Fiona says. "Keegan speaks highly of you, lass."

Keegan?

I blink, not sure what to say, but before I can come up with any words, the door opens, and people start filing in.

All I can do is stand back and watch in awe.

Anastasia and Kane arrive, looking adorable in color-coordinated outfits. I overheard Stasia telling Maggie a few days ago that she had to talk Kane into their attire, but now I can see why she did. They look fantastic.

My jaw hits the floor when I see Will Montgomery walk in. I've watched Will play for the Seattle football team for as long as I can remember. He's a megastar, and he's related to Anastasia?

More and more people file in. I recognize Amelia

Montgomery, the face and name behind the super successful makeup brand. I've watched her YouTube makeup tutorials for years.

But then my heart stops.

Literally stops beating in my chest.

I'm pretty sure I just died.

Still, my ghost watches as Leo Nash, the frontman for the rock group Nash, walks through the door and hugs Will's wife.

The man whose posters lined my walls as a teenager, whose concerts I never missed, is standing less than twenty feet away from me.

Leo. Fucking. Nash.

"Izzy?"

"Huh?" I turn to Maeve. "Yeah?"

"You just went white."

"I'm dead."

She follows my gaze and grins. "Yeah. I get it."

"I have to leave."

"Because Leo's here? Nah, he's really nice."

"You don't understand. I'm going to make a complete ass of myself. I'm going to do something stupid like trip, or ask him to take his shirt off, or volunteer to have his babies or something."

"Pretty sure he's used to that."

I turn to leave and run right into a brick wall.

I look up to find Keegan smiling down at me, his hands on my shoulders to steady me. And just like that, my body heats, my heart pounds, and I realize this visceral reaction to Keegan's nearness is much more intense than the reaction I had to seeing my teenage crush.

"Are you okay, then, Izzy?"

"Sure." I swallow hard. "I mean, yeah."

"She has a mild—and by mild I mean *huge*—crush on Leo."

Keegan's eyes narrow on my face, and I feel my cheeks flush.

"I used to," I correct her.

"Sure, that's why your face went white, and you just volunteered to have his babies."

The muscle in Keegan's jaw tics. If I didn't know better, I'd say he's mad. Or jealous.

But that's just wishful thinking.

"You guys didn't warn me until *right now* that I'd be meeting celebrities. People that I've watched and admired for *years.* On top of that, it's a family party, and I do *not* belong here."

"Come with me."

Keegan takes my hand and leads me out of the main bar area, past the kitchen door, and into his office. He shuts the door behind us and turns to me.

"Take a deep breath."

I do as instructed, and while it does help me feel a little better, my pulse is still off the charts.

Though it has nothing to do with Leo Nash.

"Let's get something straight right now, Izzy. Wait, what is Izzy short for?"

I blink quickly, surprised by the sudden change in conversation. "I'm sorry, what?"

"What is your name short for? Elizabeth?"

"Isabella," I reply and watch as Keegan clenches his fists and then slides his hands into his pockets. "Why?"

"Because I've wondered since the day I met you." His voice is calmer now. "You belong here because my family invited you to join us. Because we enjoy your company. It's that simple, Isabella. If you're uncomfortable being here, I understand, and I can take you home. But I hope you'll stay and enjoy the day with us. There's nothing to fear here, and nothing to be uncomfortable about. The O'Callaghans and the Montgomerys are both welcoming, and I promise that in less than thirty minutes, you'll be completely at ease. It's your choice."

"No one calls me Isabella," I mutter, still stuck on the way my name sounded coming from his lips.

"If you don't like it, I won't either."

"No, I like it."

He waits for my answer. "I'll stay."

I follow Keegan out of the office in time to see Luke Williams, the star from so many movies and shows when I was young, walk into the pub with none other than Starla, an amazing pop star that I'm more than obsessed with. I round on Keegan. "Really?"

"That's the last one," he says with a laugh.

The next thing I know, I'm standing next to Anastasia, and she leans in to whisper to me. "Are you okay?"

"Yeah. Your family is ridiculously intimidating."

She laughs and then nods as she looks around the room. "I can see that. I've had a long time to get used to who my family marries and who we bring into the fold. It's a lot. But, behind the public personas, they're just regular people. I promise."

"There's no way Leo Nash is regular people," I reply. "Is there any chance he'll take his shirt off?"

"I mean, we could spill something on him, on accident of course, and then he'll *have* to take it off."

We're giggling when Maeve, Maggie, and Lexi join us.

"What are you laughing at?" Lexi asks. Anastasia happily shares the story, much to my horror.

"I'm just kidding," I insist.

"I'm not," Stasia counters.

"You have to meet him." Maggie takes my hand and leads me to the other side of the room where Leo is chatting with four other men, all of whom could rival the O'Callaghans in the looks department.

And that's saying a lot.

"Hey, guys, I want to introduce you to Izzy. She's new here. Izzy, this is Caleb, Matt, Isaac, Nate, and Leo."

All of the guys smile at me. Three of them are definitely brothers. The one named Nate is sexy in a way I've only ever read about in romance novels.

And then there's Leo.

Jesus, Mary, and Joseph, he's even hotter up close.

"Nice to meet you," Leo says and offers me his hand.

He wants to touch me.

"I'm going to be brutally honest here," I say, rather than accept his hand. "I'm about to embarrass myself *really* bad."

"How so?" Leo asks, his head cocked with interest.

"I'm a big fan." I swallow hard, shocked that any sound came out at all. "I've seen every tour. I love your music. In fact, it's what got me through some really rough patches in my life. Including the day I walked out on my wedding and drove all the way here from central Oregon. But now I'm just babbling."

"Not mad about this babble," he says.

"Big fan," I repeat.

"She wants you to take your shirt off."

My eyes feel like they're going to pop out of my sockets as I elbow Maggie in the stomach.

"Ignore her."

"No, she really does."

Leo laughs, and then, with a slight shrug, he just reaches over his shoulder and peels his black t-shirt over his head like it's no big thing at all.

"Sweet baby Jesus," I breathe. "Sorry. That was completely inappropriate. It's the tattoos. Those stars on your hips—"

"Are delicious," a petite blonde says as she joins us with a smile. She wraps her arm around Leo's waist. "Trust me, I agree."

"This is Samantha, Leo's wife." Maggie introduces us.

"Well, now I've gone and done it. I am so embarrassed. Please know I didn't mean any disrespect."

"It's okay. The tattoos are something to write home about," Samantha replies. "Did I hear that you walked out on your own wedding?"

"Yeah." I sigh as Leo slips his shirt back over his head. Which is good. Because if he kept it off, I wouldn't be able to think. "It's a long story."

"I have a feeling this is going to be a long party."

THE PAST MONTH has felt like something out of a rom-com movie. Between how it all began, finding this pub, meeting these people, and the party a few days ago, more has transpired in the past four weeks than in the past four years of my life.

There's never a dull moment.

Samantha Nash ended up giving me her number so we could have lunch together sometime. Leo ended up teasing me the rest of the day about taking his shirt off. The whole atmosphere was easy and laid-back as everyone laughed and ate, and then we watched as Stasia unwrapped gifts and cried from gratitude and hormones.

It was a day I won't soon forget.

"How are you feeling, Izzy?" Fiona asks when I

come into the kitchen to place an order for one of my tables.

"Oh, I'm doing very well, thank you. And you?"

"I'm fit as a fiddle," Fiona replies. Since they've been in town, she and Tom have worked at the pub almost every day, Tom pulling taps and Fiona in the kitchen. They said it's like old times. "What can I get you?"

I read her the order, then clip the paper to the little metal stand so she can reference it if she needs to before turning to leave.

But then I turn back to her. "Fiona?"

"Yes, dear."

I want to ask some questions about Keegan. I want to ask what he was like as a child and so much more.

But at the end of the day, it's none of my business.

So, I shake my head. "It's nothing. I'll be back in a few."

Fiona waves me off, and I return to the bar. I've just approached a table to take their order, when I hear my name being called from across the room.

The hair on the back of my neck stands on end.

No.

My fears are realized when I turn around and see my mother standing by the bar. And next to her is *Troy's* mother.

Both glare daggers at me.

"What are you doing here?" I ask as I approach them.

"We're here to collect you," Mom replies. "Get your things. Let's go."

"I'm not going anywhere."

I see Keegan approach out of the corner of my eye, but I hold my hand up to stop him. He has no idea the wrath these women would rain down on him if he dared to interrupt.

"Oh, yes you are," Mom says. "You're coming home. You've had your little vacation. Now it's time for you to get back to your life. You need to ask Troy to take you back and make things right, Izzy."

"No."

"He'll forgive you," Lita insists. "My son isn't unreasonable. Just explain to him that you got nervous, and that you're better now. He'll be fine."

"Absolutely not."

I turn to walk away, but my mother grabs my arm and spins me back around.

"That's exactly what you'll do. You're finished embarrassing this family. We will plan a new wedding, and you'll marry Troy."

I shake my head. "I didn't plan the first wedding. I didn't even pick out my dress. I *hated* that thing. In fact, until I walked out of that wedding, I'd never done what *I* wanted a day in my life."

"So, what? You're just going to *leave*? Your father will unfreeze your assets and move a million dollars into your account tonight. You'll have your lifestyle back. You and Troy can move into the beautiful home he's having built."

"I don't want any money. I'm making my *own* money. And I don't care about the lifestyle. I certainly don't want Troy."

"You listen to me." Mom gets in my face, her breaths coming fast with anger. "You get your pathetic little ass in that car and go home with us, or you'll never see me again. Troy is the best man you could ever hope to marry."

"He hit me!" I yell at her, right in her face. "He fucking *hit* me, Mother. And now I've learned he's most likely been fucking anything with two legs for a long damn time. I'm not a punching bag—literally or otherwise."

"That's just how men are," Mom says, pure pity in her expression. "They cheat, and they'll smack you around if you step out of line. But the lifestyle and the perks are worth it."

"No. Not to me. I don't want to be you, Mom. I *won't* be you. Ever."

"You ungrateful little bitch."

"Whoa, now." Fiona steps in, all five feet of her, her face red with fury. "We don't speak to our children that way where I come from. Izzy has said her piece. She's a grown woman, with the choice to stay or go."

Mom doesn't even spare Fiona a glance before she spins and marches out of the bar.

Lita's face is white as she crosses to me.

"I'm sorry," she says. "I didn't raise my boy to be like that. And neither did his father. *Your* dad might act like that, and your mother is numb to it, and callous about it, but we don't behave that way in our family. I'm sorry that happened to you. And I'm so glad you've moved on. Good luck to you, Izzy."

Lita leaves, and I turn around to find the pub perfectly quiet, all eyes on me.

Without thinking, I turn and run through the bar and up the back staircase to Keegan's apartment. I can't believe that just happened, and in front of all those people. People I've come to care about and even *love.*

Keegan charges in right behind me, and I spin around when the door closes.

"I'm so sorry. I know I don't live here anymore, and that this isn't appropriate, but I had to get out of there. I'm just so *embarrassed.*"

He shakes his head. "You have nothing to be embarrassed about, Isabella. That was the strongest, sexiest thing I've ever witnessed in my life."

He immediately crosses to me, frames my face in his hands, and lowers his mouth to mine. This isn't a gentle or comforting kiss.

It's lust-filled and possessive and knocks me back on my heels. I have to hold onto his arms so I don't fall on my ass.

Keegan's lips are soft but confident as they roam over mine. His hands glide down my arms and snake around to my ass, holding on tightly.

I hear myself moan against his mouth as I lean into him and plunge my fingers into his thick, dark hair.

Finally, after a few long moments of being locked together, Keegan pulls back so we can both catch our breath.

"I'm not sorry about that."

"Good. It would suck if you were."

"I've wanted to kiss you for weeks." He swallows hard and tips his forehead to mine. "It's been hell keeping my hands to myself."

"Why did you?"

"You were a stranger. What if you decided to go back home and get married? What if you were a con artist? What if you sued me for sexual harassment?" His accent is driving me wild.

"None of those things will happen."

"And thank Christ for it."

CHAPTER 5

~KEEGAN~

$\mathcal{N}$ow that I've started kissing her, I never want to stop. I didn't lie before. It was hell staying away from her all these weeks, telling myself that helping her out was enough.

But it wasn't nearly enough.

Listening to her laugh, watching her silly dance when she's eating something delicious, and being near her all the time, day in and day out, slowly killed me inside. I thought it would be easier on me when she moved in with Maggie. That I might start to lose interest. Out of sight, out of mind and all that.

I was wrong. I've missed having her in the flat, and I still see her almost every day. There is no out of sight, out of mind.

And tonight, when she stood in my pub and was strong enough to stand up to her mother, it only intensified my attraction to her.

No, she has nothing at all to be embarrassed about.

"I guess we should go back to work," she murmurs. For the first time in as long as I can remember, work is the last thing on my mind.

But she's right. I have a pub full of customers to see to.

"Before we go,"—I brush my knuckles down her soft cheek—"I'd like to take you out. On a real date. Tomorrow."

"I happen to have tomorrow night off," she says. "But you—"

"My da's in town, remember? He'll love nothing more than to be in charge for an evening."

"Well then, you have yourself a date."

She grins, and I can't help myself. I kiss her again, softer and gentler this time until my brain buzzes, and my cock gets hard.

"Spaghetti," I whisper.

"Are you hungry?" she asks.

"I need to think of things to calm down before I say fuck the pub and carry you into my bedroom to have my way with you."

Her blue eyes dance with awareness. "I like spaghetti. I think tacos are my favorite, though."

"Hard or soft shell?"

"Hard." She grins. "With extra cilantro."

"I hate cilantro. It tastes like soap."

"Oh, you're one of those unfortunate souls with weird tastebuds."

I chuckle and shake my head. "Come on. We have work to do. Unless you'd rather go home for the night."

"No." She squares her shoulders. "Like you said, we have work to do. My mother doesn't have the privilege of interfering in my life anymore."

I follow her down to the pub, relieved when no one stands to make a big deal out of the earlier scene. We easily slip back into our roles, me pulling taps, and Izzy seeing to her tables. My da offers me a wink as he pulls the handle for the Guinness.

"Everything okay, then?"

"It is."

And that's all that's said about it for the rest of the evening.

"GOOD MORNING, MY LOVE," Ma says as she and Da walk into the pub the next morning. Despite a long workday yesterday, they're both fresh as can be and look ready to start another busy day.

"And a good morning to you." I kiss Ma's cheek and then hug my father. "You do know that you don't have to come in every single day. You can enjoy your time here on the island without working it away."

"We enjoy it," Ma replies. "And I want to get a batch of apple muffins into the oven this morning for you."

"I don't want you to work too hard."

She pats my cheek and then saunters off to the

kitchen. "Don't you worry about me, Keegan. I'm doing exactly what I want to do."

"And she always does," Da says with a smile as he watches her walk away. "I'm going to Shawn's in a bit to help him with a project at the house. But your mother wanted to come in and get some baking done and start on the stew and meat pies."

"There's nothing like having Ma in the kitchen," I admit. "Maggie's wonderful, and her stew is delicious, but it isn't the same. Don't ever tell her I said that."

Da laughs and pats me on the shoulder. "I understand your meaning, son. Fiona has a way with food. I think it's the love she pours into it. She's been looking forward to being here for weeks, just so she can spend her days back there. But don't worry, I'm keeping an eye on her. If I think she's overextending herself, I'll say so."

"I know. And now I'll sound like a hypocrite because I need to ask you a favor."

"Anything, if it's in my power. You know that."

"I need you to cover the bar for me tonight."

His brow furrows in surprise. "Is everything okay?"

"Yes, everything's fine. I'm just taking Izzy out on a date."

His brows climb. "I'm sorry, am I speaking with Keegan O'Callaghan? My second eldest son?"

I laugh and reach for a bottle of orange juice, then pour myself a glass. "One and the same, yes."

"This is unusual for you."

"If you'd rather not cover the shift, I can ask Shawn to do it."

"I didn't say that, did I?" He crosses his arms and watches me. "I like her."

I take a sip of juice. "I do, too."

"She has a backbone and an honest face. And she's kind."

"She is those things," I agree. "But don't go marrying us off quite yet, old man. This is just a date."

"If you're taking the evening away from the pub to court her, I'd say it's not *just* anything at all. But I'll mind my own. Your mother likes her, too, in case you were wondering."

"Ma likes everyone."

"Oh, she had some choice words to say last night about Izzy's ma, I'll tell you that. And, no, she doesn't like everyone when it comes to her children. She really didn't like that girl you dated in high school. What was her name?"

"You know her name was Amber. And, yes, I remember that Ma didn't like her."

"Do you have something special planned for tonight?"

"Dinner. The weather's been nice, so maybe a picnic."

"Well, enjoy yourself."

"You're not going to tell me that it's a bad idea to date an employee?"

He shakes his head. "I was married to my employee

the entire time I ran this business, and we did just fine. You're a smart man with a good head on his shoulders."

I can smell the apple muffins baking in the kitchen, and my stomach growls.

"Are you going to stay for muffins?"

"Of course. Let's go see how much longer they have to bake."

I HAVEN'T BEEN nervous about picking up a date since I was in high school. And if anyone asked, I'd say I'm not nervous now. That's just ridiculous.

I rub my hands down my jeans' legs after I cut the truck's engine and take a deep breath. The flowers on the seat next to me are fresh and smell great as I pick them up and get out of the vehicle to walk up to Maggie's door.

Someone flings it open before I can knock, and my baby sister stands before me with a smug grin on her lips.

"For me? You shouldn't have."

"You're a pain in my arse."

"I've been doing the Lord's work since 1994." She winks and opens the door wide so I can step inside. Izzy is just making her way down the stairs.

My tongue sticks to the roof of my mouth.

Thank Christ she doesn't wear this sort of outfit at

the pub. I'd never be able to hold a conversation with a customer or remember an order again.

She's in a simple summer dress, but it's red, has the tiniest hint of straps on her shoulders, and flows to mid-thigh.

My fingers itch to brush her skin there, and under the skirt, leading to the glories that lie beneath.

"He's speechless," Maggie says with a laugh. "That doesn't happen often."

"And that's the truth of it," I agree without any embarrassment at all. "I brought these for you."

"Oh, how pretty. Thank you." Izzy buries her nose in the pink roses and sniffs them delicately. "I'll just put them in some water."

"I can do that," Maggie interrupts. "You two go have fun. I won't even tease Keegan anymore."

"I don't believe that."

"Well, anymore *today*," she amends and disappears into the kitchen with Izzy's flowers.

"Shall we go?" I hold out my hand for Izzy's.

"Absolutely." She slips her hand into mine. I lead her out to the truck and open the door for her. Within just a few minutes, we're driving away from Maggie's house. "It smells really good in here."

"I brought dinner with me. I hope you're hungry."

"Starving."

"You look beautiful."

She turns that bright smile on me, and I feel my

breath catch. Jesus, Mary, and Joseph, no woman has ever tied me up in knots like this one does.

I pull into a parking space and turn to Izzy. "Wait for me."

"Okay."

I hop out of the truck, retrieve the basket from the backseat, and then circle the hood to open the door for my date.

"This is a gorgeous spot," she says as I help her down and lead her over the grass toward the cliffs that look out over the Pacific Ocean.

"It's a place I come to when I need to clear my head," I admit and set the basket on a picnic table. "Lucky for us the breeze isn't too bad today."

"I've noticed it gets pretty windy here," she observes and sits on the bench across from me. "It's because of the ocean."

"It is, yes. And in the winter, it can cut right through you. But it's a lovely day today, and I thought we could enjoy the fresh air—and your tacos."

"Tacos?" She claps her hands and dances in her seat.

"That's right, and I brought some extra cilantro for you."

"You know, I do enjoy a man who pays attention." She rests her chin in her hand and watches me unpack the basket with a soft smile on her lovely face. "It's a trait that's rarer than you'd expect."

"If you want to get to know someone, it's best to listen when they speak." I pour two margaritas into plastic glasses and set one in front of her. "I'm sorry, I can't rim the glass with salt."

"Oh, this will do nicely, thank you. I didn't think you made margaritas."

"I don't serve them at the pub, no, but I know *how* to make them." I wink and take a sip of the sweet drink, then pull out a bag of chips and sides of salsa, queso, and guacamole. "Let's start with the appetizer, shall we?"

"These are *fresh* chips. Not store-bought," Izzy says in awe as she takes one, along with a big scoop of queso and takes a bite. "Where did you find this?"

"I know the owner of the Mexican restaurant in town." I eat a chip myself and nod in satisfaction. "He set us up for dinner."

"This is seriously delicious. I might have a cheese problem."

"Are you lactose intolerant?"

"No, as in I'm addicted to cheese. I'm quite sure it was invented just for me."

"Cheese is delicious."

"What's your favorite food?" she asks.

"I suppose pizza. I know that sounds boring, but when I was growing up, pizza was for special occasions, not something eaten on a regular basis. In fact, we didn't eat out much at all because Ma loves to cook and fed us all so much."

"Well, you know I love pizza, too. I guess I just love junk food. It's no wonder I can't get rid of the curves."

"And what's wrong with your curves, Isabella?"

She blinks at me and then shrugs a shoulder as she looks down at the chip in her hand. "Nothing, I suppose."

"Did someone tell you that you shouldn't have curves?"

"Look, I don't like talking about my ex because I'm on a date with you, and it's kind of rude, but yeah. He reminded me almost daily that I shouldn't eat whatever was in my hand at the time and that I needed to get to the gym."

I shift in my seat, utterly pissed at the man she almost married. "I think you should eat whatever pleases you, as long as you throw a stalk of broccoli or a carrot in there once in a while. And you get plenty of exercise in your job. I like your curves, love."

Her cheeks darken, and she narrows her eyes at me. "Thanks. I used to just tell him that I'm a girl, and if he didn't like curves, he was batting for the wrong team."

I can't help myself. I laugh out loud, absolutely delighted with her. "And that's the truth if I've ever heard it. I like your sass, Isabella."

"Well, that's good because it's not going anywhere." She sighs, and I can see she's ready for the entrée, so I reach into the basket and pull out a half-dozen tacos and some chicken fajitas.

"This is a *lot* of food."

"I didn't know which you'd like better, so I just got a little of each."

"That's a lot of each, but I'm not complaining." She reaches for a taco and takes a bite. "Jesus, I just found my new favorite restaurant."

"I'll take you in there sometime. Javier is a master in the kitchen."

"Obviously." She takes another bite. "So, what were you like as a kid?"

"In what sense?"

"Were you shy? Nerdy? A jock?"

I laugh and pile some chicken onto a tortilla. "I guess I was a nerdy jock. I liked sports a lot. Mostly baseball and basketball, although I also played football in high school."

"Definitely a jock."

"But I also like to read, and I did well in school."

"A well-rounded kid, then."

"I guess so. What about you?"

"I definitely wasn't shy. I was the social butterfly. I had lots of friends, but no super-close friends. Does that make sense?"

"Yes."

"And I was totally a cheerleader. I know most people make fun of girls who cheer, but I have to tell you, it was hard work."

"I don't make fun of it," I reply.

"And then I went to college and wanted to be a meteorologist on television."

I take a sip of my margarita. "I remember you

saying that before. So, you wanted to be a weather girl?"

"More than anything. Still do, actually. I love the weather. I study it still and keep track of what's going on and where. It's actually quite interesting."

"So, why don't you do that, then?"

"Because my parents wanted me to work for the family business. Because of that, I had to minor in business in college. As soon as I finished, I started working at my dad's office. It was soul-sucking."

"And why did your parents have so much say over what you did with your life?"

Her mouth opens and closes twice, and then she gazes out at the ocean for a moment. "Because they held the purse strings. And let me tell you, that's not easy to admit. Some of it was also guilt. I felt like I *should* be a good daughter and help them."

"And now?"

"Now I see that it was a way for them to control me. I was there because I was dependent on them for my income and wanted their approval. They even chose Troy *for* me because his father and mine are friends. And he's wealthy. The relationship looked really good on paper. I'm not often asked for my opinion or for what I want."

"And what *do* you want?"

"This." She waves her hand over the table and gestures to the town. "I want to make my own living, have my own friends, and go on dates with my handsome boss."

I smile at her. "All of those things sound good to me."

The sun sets over the water as Izzy and I finish our meal, and I pack the leftovers in the basket.

"Let's walk over here," I suggest and take her hand in mine to lead her down a path to the edge of the cliff where a bench sits. "Have a seat."

"This might be the best view in the world."

"I couldn't agree more."

She glances my way and sees that I'm looking at her. "You're charming."

"I'm not, no." I tuck a piece of blond hair behind her ear. "But I'm taken with you, Isabella, and I find myself wanting to be near you more often than not."

"Is that a bad thing?"

"Not from where I'm sitting."

I lean in and kiss her cheek. I want to pull her to me and claim her mouth with mine, but we aren't the only two in the park, and I don't want her to miss the sunset.

"Watch."

I point west, and we sit in silence as the sun slips behind the horizon.

"I HAD A LOT OF FUN TONIGHT," Izzy says as I walk her up the steps to the front door. "And I'm not just saying that because it's customary when a date is over."

"I enjoyed myself, as well." I brace my hand on the doorjamb next to her head and lean in to brush my lips gently over hers. "I'd like to see you again. And often."

"I'd like that, too." Her voice is breathy, and her hands grip the front of my shirt as I take the kiss deeper, enjoying the last few moments I have with her.

Suddenly, the porch light comes on, startling us both.

"Thought you'd like to see what you're doing out there," Maggie calls through the door.

Izzy laughs.

I scowl.

"Maybe you should go ahead and move back in with me so I don't have my baby sister as a gatekeeper every time I want to see you."

"Don't be grouchy," Maggie yells through the door.

"Get the hell away from this door before I take you over my knee, Mary Margaret."

I hear laughter as she walks away. Izzy smiles up at me.

"Thank you for dinner, and the incredible view. And the conversation. I was going to ask your mom about you, but it's better to get the information from the source."

"I think we have plenty more to learn about each other."

"I agree. We have time."

I nod, kiss her once more, and then turn to leave while my feet can still carry me away. I wait in the truck until she's safely inside, and then I drive the short distance to the pub.

I could go relieve my da and take care of the bar for the rest of the night. It's not even ten o'clock.

But I don't.

I promised myself a night off, and I'm going to take it.

So, I climb the steps to my flat and sit on the couch. Pulling my phone out of my pocket, I bring up Izzy's number.

Me: *I'll be there to pick you up at 8:00 a.m.*

I smile at the three bubbles bouncing on the screen as she types her reply.

Izzy: *I'll be ready. Good night, handsome.*

CHAPTER 6

"Your brother is taking me out to breakfast," I inform Maggie as I swing into the kitchen and pour myself a little glass of orange juice. "He should be here any minute."

"Fun." She watches me speculatively.

"What's on your mind?"

"Nothing." She shrugs and takes my glass to have a sip. "You didn't tell me much about your date last night."

"And I probably won't tell you much about it today."

She huffs out a breath and scowls. "You can trust me, you know."

"Oh, trust isn't the issue. I had a good time. And I'm keeping the rest to myself for now. If I didn't enjoy myself, I wouldn't let him take me out for breakfast today."

"I guess that's true," she says as the doorbell rings.

I hurry and open the door to find Keegan, hair damp from his shower, wearing a dark green T-shirt and faded blue jeans.

My mouth waters.

"Good morning," he greets with a grin. "You look fantastic."

"As do you. I'm ready when you are."

"I want to go," Maggie says as she joins us. "I'm hungry."

Keegan's eyes narrow on his sister. I smile. I don't mind if she joins us at all.

"Come on, then," he agrees, and the three of us climb into Keegan's truck. He drives us to the edge of town to his favorite diner. Most of the tables are empty as we're shown to a booth on the edge of the room. Keegan slides in next to me, and Maggie sits across from us.

"You guys are cute together," she says.

"Are you going to be a jerk the whole time we're here, or can you behave like a regular human being, Mary Margaret?"

"I'm not a jerk, you jerk. I simply said you're cute. And you are."

"What can I get you?" the waitress asks.

"I'm going to have the breakfast tacos. To go," Maggie adds. "I just came to torment my brother. Can you add extra salsa on the side and some hash browns? Oh, and a cinnamon roll."

"How many are you eating for?" Keegan asks.

"You don't have to leave," I rush to assure Maggie.

"I'm gonna walk over to Maeve's and see what she's up to. Really."

I order the pancakes, and Keegan gets his usual oatmeal. When the food is delivered, with Maggie's bagged up and ready to go, she stands and offers me a smile.

"In all seriousness, you *are* cute together. I like it. And don't forget, we're having lunch tomorrow with Maeve."

"Oh, I won't forget. I'm excited."

Maggie grins and takes her food. Before she makes it out the door, a tall man approaches her.

Maggie frowns.

"Who's that?" I ask Keegan.

"Cameron," he replies, watching them with narrowed eyes.

"Who's Cameron?"

"Kane's best friend. A friend of the whole family, really, as they've been close since they were small boys."

"He looks at Maggie like she hung the moon." I watch in fascination as Maggie's face turns mutinous, then shuts down altogether. She says something I can't hear, then shakes her head and walks away.

Cameron watches her with so much longing, it makes my heart hurt.

"I wish they'd just admit that they're meant for each other," Keegan mutters.

"Oh, he knows," I assure him. "That poor man is in love with her. I think your sister's being stubborn."

"She wouldn't be Mary Margaret if she wasn't being stubborn." Keegan waves at Cameron as the other man walks across the room and stands next to our booth. "Good morning to you, mate."

"It was," Cameron says with a sigh and glances back to where Maggie was. She's now gone.

"I didn't know you were back in town," Keegan interjects.

"I'm here for a couple of weeks." Cameron slides his hands into his back pockets. "I'd like to have a talk with you and Kane. Shawn, too, whenever you have time."

"We'll make time," Keegan says. "Is everything okay?"

"Yes, nothing to worry about." He glances down at me and smiles. "Sorry, I'm rude. Cameron."

He reaches out to shake my hand. "Izzy."

"Nice to meet you, Izzy." He turns back to Keegan. "Just shoot me a text when you guys have a minute."

"You got it."

Cameron nods and then walks away. He picks up a to-go order from the long counter near the kitchen and then leaves the diner.

"He seems nice." I take a bite of my pancakes.

"He's the best. Like a brother to us." Keegan shifts in the seat and rests his arm on the bench behind me, leaving his oatmeal untouched. "Do you want me to shift to the other side?"

"No, this is cozy." I grin up at him. His green eyes deepen as his gaze drops to my lips. I know he's thinking about kissing me.

I've thought of little else since the last time he did it last night.

The man is an extraordinary kisser.

But before his lips can descend on mine, the waitress appears. "Everything okay here?"

"Yes," Keegan says without looking at her. Instead of kissing me, here in front of the whole town, he turns and digs into his oatmeal.

"What are your plans for today?" I ask him as I take another bite.

"After we finish breakfast, I have to go to the pub for a delivery. I'll be unpacking bottles until it's time to open for the day."

"Do you want help?"

He shakes his head. "You don't have to do that."

"Well, I'm not asking to clock in, I'm asking if you'd like me to come give you a hand so we can hang out together *and* be productive at the same time."

"If you come help, you'll clock in."

I roll my eyes and shrug a shoulder. "Fine. But if you'd rather not, that's okay, too. I'm not forcing myself on you."

He laughs and pushes away his empty bowl. "Let's try this again."

"Okay, do you want some help today?"

"Sure, that would definitely be better than doing it alone."

"See, that wasn't hard."

"WHOA." We're in the storeroom, staring at a mountain of boxes. "This is some delivery."

"Every week at this time." He takes a box down from the top, his muscles straining with the effort, and my mouth goes dry.

Dear Lord above, I've never seen anything like him before. The broad shoulders and defined arms are a sight to behold.

It's borderline ridiculous.

"I'll take the boxes out behind the bar and show you where to unload them, if you like."

"Sounds perfect." I follow him out of the storeroom to the bar, and he sets the boxes down in front of where he wants them.

"Beer bottles go in the cooler. I pull out the existing ones and put the new ones to the back, then the older ones in front."

"Makes sense."

"The extra liquor goes in the cabinet under here."

"Got it. Looks pretty self-explanatory."

"Now, I have one *very* important question, lass."

"Okay, what is it?"

"What kind of music do you prefer? We can't do this in silence, can we?"

"No, that wouldn't work at all. Hmm… I guess just regular pop music."

He pulls out his phone and taps the screen. A few seconds later, music comes through the speakers in the corners of the room.

"Fancy."

"I like music," he replies. "This is satellite radio. If the station starts to irritate you, just let me know."

As I unpack boxes, Keegan walks back and forth between the bar and the storeroom, carrying the bottles.

"Why don't you use a dolly?"

"I don't belong to a gym," he says as he sets another heavy box down. "I don't have the time. So, this is my exercise. I won't bring them all out today, some will stay back there, and I'll haul more throughout the week as I need them."

"Well, it works."

"Why do you say that?"

I sit back on my haunches and blow a piece of hair out of my eyes. "I don't know if you've noticed, but your muscles are impressive."

"It's my muscles you like, is it?"

"They don't hurt."

A slow song comes over the speakers, and Keegan holds his hand out for mine. "Let's take a break."

"We just started."

"I'm the boss here, and I'm telling us to take a break." He pulls me to my feet and leads me out to the small dance floor in front of the stage. He loops one arm around my back and holds the other against his chest as we sway back and forth to the music.

I can't help myself.

I lean in and rest my cheek on his firm chest, giving in to the sway of our bodies and the gentle beat of the music as John Legend sings about you and I.

Keegan's heart beats strong beneath my ear.

His lips are buried in my hair as he kisses my head.

And with his arms and scent wrapped around me, I'm completely caught up in the moment, in this potent man.

Could I be falling for him? Or am I just thrilled at the idea of being treated so nicely? Am I grateful that he took me in without a resume or a background check and came to my rescue?

Or is it both?

"I have a feeling you're thinking way too hard about something," he murmurs. He tips my chin up with his finger and lowers his lips toward mine.

This kiss is different from any of the others. It's lazy and slow, just like the song.

His hand travels down my back to my butt. He clenches it there, and I lean into him harder.

Suddenly, the door opens, and the moment is lost.

"Whoops," Shawn says with a grin. "Sorry, you two.

I have to get a few things ready in the kitchen. Ma called, and she's not feeling well this morning."

I brush my hands over my face as Keegan pulls back.

"What's wrong with Ma?" he asks.

"She didn't elaborate, just asked me to cover the kitchen today. It's not a problem for me."

I clear my throat and walk back behind the bar to continue unloading boxes. "Good morning, Shawn."

"And good morning to you, Izzy." He winks and walks into the kitchen.

I blow out a long breath.

The man sure can kiss.

"WE CAN'T DRINK MUCH, we have to work tonight," Maggie reminds Maeve as her sister pours us each a glass of wine.

"I'm working tonight, too," Maeve replies. "Keegan roped me into a shift. I don't really mind."

"You haven't been working at the pub much," Maggie says as she takes her wine.

"No. Thanks to Izzy here." Maeve smiles at me. "Thanks for that, by the way. I'm able to take more evening appointments to show houses. You know, my actual job."

"I've always been so fascinated by real estate," I say as I reach for a slice of pizza. We decided to meet at

Maeve's house for lunch so we could have quiet and would be able to chat without anyone else listening. "I love looking at houses."

"You and a lot of other people," she says. "I can't tell you how many calls I get from people just wanting to look at a house with no intention of actually buying it."

"I bet that happens a lot with the big, fancy houses," I say.

"If it's over a million, I have a stipulation that I'll only show to people who are pre-approved for a mortgage. That usually helps carve out the lookie-loos."

"Good idea." I spear some lettuce with my fork and take a bite.

"I don't get to talk to you as often as Maggie does," Maeve says and sips her wine. "So I'm just going to get to the point. What's going on with you and Keegan? Shawn said he walked in on you two making out in the bar yesterday."

"What?" Maggie exclaims and stares at me in shock. "You don't tell me *anything!*"

"It was just a kiss," I insist and feel my cheeks flush. "And I'm not used to confiding in people. As you could probably tell, my friends from *before* weren't exactly good ones."

"Have any of them reached out to you?" Maeve asks.

"Only one, to rub Troy's trip to Aruba in my face."

"Bitches," she mutters.

"Well, you can confide in us. Or Stasia and Lexi. We

won't tell anyone anything you don't want told," Maggie insists.

"I like him a lot," I admit and stare down at my half-eaten slice of pepperoni pizza. "He's sweet and thoughtful. He listens to me. And you may not want to hear this, but your brother can *kiss.*"

"Ew." Maggie scrunches up her nose. "TMI."

"Be careful there," Maeve advises. "He's definitely all of those things— Well, I wouldn't know about the kissing, but you know what I mean. But he's also very married to that pub."

"She's right," Maggie agrees. "He's a great guy, but he doesn't really date anyone for very long. It's not that he's a player, really, it's just that he gets absorbed in running his business, and the girl gets pushed to the back burner."

"And you don't deserve to be the back-burner girl," Maeve adds. "You're a front and center, rolling boil kind of girl."

I stare at both of them. "Are you warning me away from your brother?"

"No, not at all. Actually, we really like you for him. I wasn't kidding when I said you're cute together." Maggie grins at me. "We just want you to be aware of what you're getting yourself into."

"Basically, a good time without long-term strings attached," I say.

"Yeah, I think that's probably an accurate assumption," Maeve says. "So, have fun with him, but don't fall in love with him."

What if it's too late for that?

"Thanks for the advice, you guys."

"I hope we didn't hurt your feelings," Maeve insists. "Because I really do like you, and I hope I get to know you even better. And Keegan is a good guy. He doesn't try to hurt anyone."

"No, I'm sure he doesn't."

This gives me a lot to think about.

"Okay, let's not talk about that depressing stuff anymore," Maggie says. "I want to hear more about the meteorologist thing."

"What meteorologist thing?" Maeve asks.

"Izzy went to school to be a weather girl."

Maeve's eyes widen, and her gaze flies to mine. "Really? Why aren't you doing that?"

"It's a long, sad story," I say with a laugh, but give them the CliffsNotes version of the tale I told Keegan the other day.

"But you're trained," Maggie adds. "Like, you *could* do it?"

"Sure."

"Show us," Maeve says.

I blink at her. "What?"

"Show us, right here. Do a mock weather report."

"Make it a dramatic winter storm report," Maggie adds, clapping her hands.

"This is fun. Okay." I jump off the stool at Maeve's

breakfast bar and rub my hands down my thighs, suddenly nervous. "I haven't done this in a little while."

"You're going to be great," Maggie insists.

I stand in front of the wall and pretend it's the green screen. "I need a key fob."

"Here," Maeve says and pulls one out of her purse, tossing it my way.

I glance off to the left as if I'm looking at a monitor and use the fob as a pretend clicker to cycle through the screens.

"Good morning to you on this chilly day. I'm sure you're already noticing that it's *cold* outside, and this weather is going to continue into tomorrow evening. As you can see here, Seattle has a high of just twenty-four degrees, and that's much colder than we're used to in the Pacific Northwest."

I go on to describe the low pressure and the forecast for the next several days. When I'm finished, both girls give me a standing ovation.

"Okay, first of all, you are *badass* at that," Maeve says.

"Yeah, why aren't you doing that for a living?" Maggie asks. "And, yes, I know because of your parents, but you can do it *now*."

"You're beautiful, and I know you'd look amazing on camera. Seriously, what would be involved in getting you into this as a regular gig?"

"There are exams to take," I reply, thinking it over. "And then I'd have to make some videos of me doing pretty much just what I did for you guys to use as an audition."

"Maybe you could get a job at one of the stations in Seattle," Maggie says.

"I doubt it. Seattle is a big market, and I don't have enough experience to get on somewhere like that. I'd probably have to start somewhere small, and then work my way up over time."

"Are you going to have to go on location in a yellow rain slicker and report in a hurricane?" Maeve asks.

"I should be so lucky," I mutter.

"You have to do this," Maggie insists. "We can help you film the video. Hell, we know Luke Williams."

"I don't think I need anything that extravagant," I say with a laugh. "But I definitely will need someone to work a camera."

"Promise you'll think about it," Maeve insists. "You looked so happy just now."

"It felt really good." I nod, the idea taking shape in my head. "I'm going to think on it."

CHAPTER 7

~IZZY~

"*I* need two pints of Guinness and a glass of whiskey on the rocks," I say as I approach the bar where Keegan's standing, talking with a customer. "I'll be back to get those in a sec. Have to put a food order in."

I don't look Keegan in the eyes as I flutter away to the kitchen, pushing through the door, almost running smack-dab into Lexi.

"Whoa. Sorry," I say with a laugh. "You okay?"

"Oh, no worries. We're always running about. We're bound to run into each other. How's your day going?"

"Good, actually." Aside from the part where Maggie and Maeve basically told me I have no chance at anything long-term with their brother. "It's busy in the pub tonight, and that makes it fun."

"I agree." She hurries back to the freezer and returns with a huge bag of fries.

"What do you have for us, Izzy?" Shawn asks. I still can't look him in the eye after he caught Keegan and I lip-locked yesterday. "Okay, let's talk about it."

I look up. "Talk about what?"

"Yesterday."

"Oh, I don't really have time for—"

"You have a minute," he says. "There's no need to be embarrassed. You're both consenting adults, Izzy."

"I know." I blow out a breath and then shrug a shoulder. Given that I've decided not to see Keegan anymore, there's no reason to be slightly embarrassed. "Okay, you're right. I'm fine."

"Well, that was easy." Shawn grins and nods toward the notebook in my hand. "What do you have for us?"

I put in my order for food and then bustle away, back to the bar where Keegan's loaded up my tray.

"Thanks."

"Hey, Izzy."

I stop and look up at him with a raised brow. "Yeah?"

"Is everything okay, lass?"

The *lass* still makes my stomach jump. Damn him. "Everything's perfectly fine."

I turn away and go back to work, seeing to my customers. Over the past few weeks, I've gotten so much better at this job. I haven't broken a glass in weeks, my feet aren't killing me, and I remember not only the customers' names but also their orders most of the time. I do still use the notebook, just in case.

I've come to feel like I belong here, and I'm not going to mess it up by getting involved with Keegan for a short-term fling, and then have to try and act like nothing happened so I can keep my job.

I'm way too old and too smart to fall into that trap.

The rest of the evening is fun and lively, with joyful Irish music and happy customers. Maggie gets up to sing a song or two with the band, and I have a bounce in my step as I make my way from table to table, enjoying the camaraderie in the bar. I even sing along with some of the songs that I'm coming to recognize.

The night flies by, and before long, Keegan is turning the lock on the door, and we're mopping floors and cleaning tables.

"It was a good night," Maggie says with a grin as she counts her tips. "Tourist season may be winding down, but our locals never let us down."

"It was fun," I agree as I toss my rag into the dirty laundry basket and glance around the bar. "I think we're done for the night."

"We're done, too," Shawn adds as he and Lexi walk out of the bar. "Hey, Maggie, can you give us a lift home? We walked over this afternoon."

"Of course." The three of them walk to the door, and just as I turn to join them, Keegan's voice, strong and firm, stops me.

"Stop."

I turn with a raised brow. "Excuse me?"

"I'd like to have a word with Izzy. You three go. I'll make sure she gets home."

"Okay, see you in a bit," Maggie says with a wave. When the three of them are gone, and the door is locked once more, Keegan turns to me with intense green eyes.

"We're going to talk about whatever it is that's bothering you, Isabella."

I raise my chin. "Nothing is bothering me."

"That's bullshit if ever I heard it."

I cross my arms over my chest. "I had a good evening. I feel pretty good. I can't think of anything at all that's wrong."

"I feel you pulling away from me," he says. "I felt the shift the second you walked into the pub this afternoon. What happened?"

I sigh, resigned to having this conversation, and hoping he doesn't fire me. Not that I think Keegan is that kind of a boss, but still.

"Look, I just think it's probably a good idea if we cool things between us. I don't want any weirdness when it's over."

"When it's over." He shifts on his feet and tucks his hands into his pockets.

"Yeah, when it's over. Your sisters told me today that you're not really the kind of guy who gets serious about someone. And I'm not saying that I want to marry you tomorrow or anything like that—trust me, I'm not ready for that—but I do deserve to be with someone who might entertain the possibility of someday wanting me to be an important part of his life. And I'm not judging you for not being that person. Not at all. I guess I was just made aware that we're very different people, and I love this job. And you and your family. So, I think it's a good idea if we go back to being friends."

I let out a breath and watch as Keegan rolls his tongue over his teeth, then nods his head and rubs his hand over his lips in agitation.

"You're mad."

"Frustrated is a better word for what I am," he says slowly. "First of all, Maeve and Mary Margaret don't speak for me. They don't know the inner workings of any of my past relationships, and they aren't psychic, so they can't read my bleeding mind. Second of all, I think this is a decision I should be a part of."

"Well, it's just—"

"I'm not finished. You had your say, so I'll have mine, as well."

I close my mouth and nod.

"Is this what you really want, Isabella? Do you want me to back off and keep my hands to meself?"

His Irish has kicked up big time with his agitation, only adding to the sexiness factor.

"Well, I—"

"Because I will, if it's what you're wanting. I won't bother you at all, and I'll be the kind and respectful boss I've always been."

That actually sounds horrible. And standing ten feet away from him, all I want is for him to pull me close and hug me. To reassure me that everything his sisters said is wrong.

I should have just talked to him rather than assume —making a mess in the process.

"I don't think that's what I want," I admit.

He crosses to me and frames my face in his hands. Immediately, I'm calmer. My hands grasp his wrists as I look up into those intense eyes.

"I should have talked to you."

"You should have, aye," he breathes. "You've already become an important part of my life, Izzy. It's only been a short time, but I look forward to my time with you, and I only crave more. Kissing you is at once heaven and hell because I want to take it further, but I don't know what you're ready for. Everything about you is a morgen's call."

"What's a morgen?" I ask softly.

"It's the Irish version of the Greek siren," he says with a grin.

"Oh, that's actually really nice." My hands move up his arms and down his sides, then fist in his plain white T-shirt. "In case you're wondering, I'm ready for much more than kissing. Although, the kissing is pretty damn hot."

"Is it, then?"

"As is your accent."

"It's my accent you like, is it?"

"That can't be the first time you've heard that."

His lips twitch, but he doesn't confirm or deny.

"So, if I invited you to stay the night with me upstairs…?"

"I'd accept."

He lifts me into his strong hold, and I wrap my arms around his neck, my fingers diving into his thick, dark hair. Our lips fuse together. He kisses me as if he's starving.

It's the sexiest thing ever.

Keegan is the sexiest man ever.

And, hell yes, I want to stay the night with him. I want to be with him, in his big bed, tumbling around naked and enjoying each other.

I have a feeling sex will take on a whole new meaning with this man.

He easily climbs the stairs to his apartment, opens the door, and carries me right through to the bedroom.

Do not pass go. Do not collect two hundred dollars.

I like his style.

I expect him to drop me onto the bed, but he sets me on my feet and takes a deep breath before reaching up and tugging my hair from its ponytail.

"I love it when your golden hair is down around your shoulders."

I shake it out and watch as Keegan's eyes darken.

"Are you just going to look at me?"

"For a moment," he says as his gaze travels the length of my body to my feet, and then moves back up to my face, leaving heat and desire in its wake. "You're so damn beautiful."

He finally reaches out and tugs my shirt from my jeans, slowly pulling it over my head. He doesn't toss it onto the floor, though. He lays it nicely over the back of a chair in the corner.

"Is this going to take a long time?"

"What?"

"Getting naked. Because you're moving rather slow, and I'm impatient."

He laughs and unfastens the button of my jeans. "It's like unwrapping a present. You can go fast and tear the paper to get to the goods—and sometimes, that's appropriate. But you can also unwrap it carefully, making sure not to damage what's underneath. It's a tease, isn't it? Wondering what you're about to uncover but enjoying the anticipation at the same time."

"Definitely a tease," I whisper as he guides my jeans over my hips and down my legs. He urges me to step out of them, then lays them carefully with my shirt. I'm standing before him in just my underwear. I move to cross my arms over my chest, but he takes my hand and kisses my knuckles.

"There's never a need to cover yourself in front of me, love. You're absolutely breathtaking."

"And you're overdressed."

I dip my hands under his T-shirt and feel the warm skin with my fingertips. His muscles ripple at my touch, making me smile.

When I get the fabric over his head, I let my eyes roam over his toned body, appreciating the lines of muscles on his torso and shoulders.

I smell his shirt, enjoying the musky scent of him before folding it and placing it on the seat of the chair.

"I'll be taking that with me," I inform him when I turn back and slide my fingers into the waistband of his jeans.

I've never done this before. In the past, sex has always been fast and frantic, in the dark. Not slow and fun.

He's already hard. He can't hide that fact, even behind the denim, and when my finger slips down just a bit farther, I can feel the tip of him.

He sucks in a breath, air hissing between his teeth.

I pop the button free and slide the zipper down. With my eyes on his, I let the jeans pool around his feet.

"Shall I fold those for you?"

Without answering, he lifts me easily onto the mattress and covers me. He takes my wrist then slips down to link our fingers and pin the back of my hand to the bed over my head as his lips travel from my ear to my collarbone, making me moan and writhe beneath him.

I'm lost, drowning in sensation.

He unclasps the front of my bra and cups my breast with his free hand. I'm a chesty girl, have always been a bit self-conscious of my breasts, but he lovingly kisses and teases my nipple until it's firm and fully awake.

"Fucking hell, you're gorgeous." His voice is strained and rough with arousal. He releases my hand so he can move farther down my body, exploring each and every inch along the way.

He nudges his way between my legs and pulls my panties to the side. The next thing I know, stars explode behind my eyes as he covers me with his mouth and does things to me that I didn't even know were possible.

I cry out, grip his hair, and ride the wave of orgasm flowing through me.

When I can breathe again, Keegan opens his nightstand and fetches a condom. With his eyes on mine, he tears the packet with his teeth and quickly sheathes himself. But he doesn't fill me right away. He tips his forehead against mine and rubs our noses together.

"Are you sure this is what you want?"

"Oh, yeah." I grin and raise my hips in invitation. "Now would be a good time."

He goes back to kissing my neck and shoulder, then drags his knuckles over the tight nipple of my left breast. Just when I think I might spontaneously combust from the lust, he urges my knees up higher around his hips and then slowly slips inside of me.

I gasp at the size of him. He clenches his eyes shut.

"Jesus, Mary, and Joseph, you're damn tight," he growls.

"You're just big," I reply, earning a half-grin. I clench my muscles, and that grin fades as he starts to move.

"I'll never last long, love." He buries his face in my neck as he moves, and each time his pubis hits my clit, I see stars all over again.

"Me, either."

"You're too sweet. Too damn good." He moves faster until he succumbs to his release, taking me over with him.

We're a tangle of sweaty limbs as we try to catch our breath. I'm not sure I can move, even if I wanted to.

But Keegan finds the strength to roll to his side, taking his weight off me, and then cups my cheek gently.

"Did I hurt you?"

"No." I kiss his palm and roll to face him. "You didn't hurt me."

I MUST HAVE FALLEN asleep because the next thing I know, someone kissing my neck and shoulder wakes me.

And Lord have mercy, it feels damn good.

"Well, hello there," I murmur and turn around to find Keegan smiling down at me.

"Good morning."

"Morning?" I sit up and push my hair out of my face. "It's *morning?*"

"Yes, ma'am. Nine a.m., in fact."

I stare at him in surprise. "It feels like I slept for like twenty minutes."

"You were *out*," he says. "I should have just let you sleep."

"No, it's okay." My phone rings, surprising me, but Keegan just goes back to kissing my shoulder.

"Ignore it." His hand dives under the covers and slips between my legs.

"Talked me into it."

He laughs and continues the delicious torture, but several seconds later, my phone rings again.

"Just ignore it."

"What if it's an emergency?"

Keegan sighs and reaches for my phone. His eyes narrow, and he answers, putting it on speaker.

"Yes, Mary Margaret?"

"Oh. If you're answering, Izzy must be with you."

"I'm here," I say. "Is everything okay?"

"That's what I was wondering. When I got up this morning and saw that you didn't come home last night, I worried."

"You knew she was with me," Keegan says.

"I'm just making sure she's safe, that's all."

"Mary Margaret." Keegan sighs as I get out of bed and reach for his T-shirt. "I know you mean well, but you're a bloody cockblocker."

I giggle as I slip the cotton over my head.

"Okay, I can take a hint," Maggie says. "See you both later."

She clicks off, and I turn to find Keegan lying on his back, his hands under his head. "Come back here."

"No way. Let's go get some breakfast. I'm starving."

"And then can we come back here?"

I shrug. "Sure."

"Promise?"

I laugh. "I promise after you feed me, we can come back here, turn off the phone, and have sex all day."

"It's a deal."

CHAPTER 8

"*W*ell, hello there," I greet my gorgeous—and very pregnant—sister-in-law. She's sitting in the sunroom at the back of the house, her hands folded over her belly, watching the water past the cliffs.

"Good morning," she says with a sweet smile. "Whales have been playing out there this morning. I was just watching."

"It's a good spot for watching. When will the wee one be here?"

"In the next week or so." She rubs her belly. "Not soon enough. I can't make my cakes anymore because I can't reach everything I need, and I can't lift them. I'm bored out of my mind, except when I'm cleaning everything because I'm *nesting.* Also, my ankles are *always* swollen. Anyway, what are you up to?"

My mind swirls with that information dump, so I shake my head and refocus.

"I came to chat with your husband, but I think this is much better for now." I sit next to her and let out a long breath. "You just can't beat this view. Reminds me of Ireland."

She smiles over at me. "That's what Kane says, too. It's why he bought this property."

I already know that, of course. I was with him the day he bought it.

"When are you going to buy yourself something like this?" she asks, surprising me.

"Well, if you'd asked me that a few months ago, I would have said that I'm content above the pub."

"And now?"

I shrug a shoulder, not sure I want to give voice to the thoughts recently filling my head. Suddenly, I think I might want more than just the pub.

"You can tell me," she insists and reaches over to pat my hand. "I'm a vault."

"Oh, that doesn't concern me."

"What *does* concern you, Keegan?"

"I suppose it's normal for a person to have a change in plans at some point in his life. I have always been absorbed in the pub, and I liked it that way."

Her lips twitch. "Do go on."

"It's nosy you are, Anastasia O'Callaghan."

She laughs and then nods her head. "True enough.

Only because I love you and I want to know how you are. Izzy seems like a special girl."

"She's that," I agree without elaborating.

"You don't have to make decisions about the future today. But it's telling that you've had a passing thought or two about what you want in the future. There's nothing to be ashamed of when it comes to wanting a home with a sweet woman."

"If I ask her to be mine,"—I have to pause to swallow hard—"I can't expect her to be content with living above the pub."

"I think she'd probably be happy there for a while," Stasia says slowly. "But if you have children, the apartment is small."

"My parents raised five children in it until Maggie was close to five years old."

"I didn't say it was impossible," she clarifies. "Just that it's small."

"This isn't the conversation I planned to have when I came here." And I need to put an end to it because I haven't even had time to wrap my head around all of these ideas for myself. I'm speaking about it out of turn.

She laughs and points to the barn about a hundred yards away, where my brother fires his glass. "He's in there."

"Is he surly today, then?"

"Isn't he always?"

"Good point. I'll go find him."

"Good luck."

"I'll need it. Kane's a horse's arse when he gets interrupted."

"I meant with Izzy," Stasia says.

I wave and walk out to the barn. It's no use knocking, he won't hear me, so I open the door and slip inside then close it behind me. Kane's across the room, dipping hot glass into water to cool it down. He's drenched in sweat, but he looks satisfied in the morning's work so far.

Once the glass is safely in a cooler, and Kane turns around, I step forward.

"Good morning."

"It is, aye," he replies. "You have good timing."

"I wouldn't have, but I sat for a chat with your lovely bride."

His face softens. I've never seen my moody, surly brother as happy as I have since he found Stasia. "And how is she, then?"

"She looks great. Says she feels fine. I suspect she's sick of being pregnant."

"You'd suspect right. She yelled at me last night for putting her in this condition, and then scowled at me when I stopped rubbing her feet. It's abused, I am. On a daily basis. But I don't think you came here to discuss my wife's pregnancy."

"I didn't, no. Is anyone using the cabin over the next few days?"

His eyes meet mine in surprise. "Not that I'm aware of."

"I didn't know if Ma and Da were up there."

"They're with Maeve," he says. "Are you planning to take a couple of days to go up there?"

I nod and then rub the back of my neck in agitation. "I know, it's unlike me."

"I'm wondering if I'm speaking to my *brother*, Keegan O'Callaghan."

"There's no need to be a wanker."

Kane grins, enjoying himself. "It's empty."

I nod and turn away.

"You could have called for that."

"You don't answer your goddamn phone," I remind him. "And I like coming out here. You have a nice property. How many acres is it?"

He props his hands on his hips and stares at me. "Do you have a fever, then?"

"Fuck off."

He laughs and shakes his head. "I have twenty acres."

"How far down the coastline does your property go?"

"Let's go out and walk it," he says, gesturing for me to follow. We walk past his house and wave at Anastasia, who's still sitting on the sunporch. "My house sits on the edge of the property. There's only about an acre that way before you hit the next owner's land, although they've never built anything there. I've thought about buying it, but I don't have a purpose for it right now. The barn sits in the middle of this five-acre patch, close enough to the house that I don't have to walk all over God's green Earth to get out there."

"So, it runs along the cliffs for a while then?"

"It does."

"Have you ever considered selling part of it?"

He stops and turns to me, his eyes—so like mine— narrowed on me. "I hadn't before. What's on your mind?"

"Just an idea that started taking shape over the past couple of weeks. If I were to buy property not attached to the pub, I'd want waterfront. But that's hard to come by on an island. Not to mention, I don't make the millions it would take to buy some of the houses here."

"Money is no object—"

"You don't pay for me, Kane." I clap him on the shoulder. "I love you for saying that, but I pay for my own."

"Stubborn arse," he mutters.

"If you would ever part with an acre or two along the cliffs, I'd buy from you and build a house there. And, maybe one day, raise a family there."

"Jesus, Keegan, what's gotten into you?"

"I asked you the same question not long ago."

He nods thoughtfully. "They'll change your world, a woman will. If that's what you want, Keegan, I'd be happy to work something out with you regarding the land."

I nod, my mind racing with ideas. "Let's talk about it again once I've had time to think on it more."

"Good idea. When are you headed to the cabin?"

"In a few hours."

He laughs loud enough to scare a dozen birds off a nearby tree. "You don't mess around when you've set your mind to something."

"It runs in the family."

BEFORE I CAN WHISK Izzy away for a few days, I need to make one more stop. I asked my sisters to meet me at Maeve's house for a little conversation.

I don't know that I've ever been angrier with my sisters, even when, at sixteen, they cut my hair when I was asleep.

I had to shave my head.

But this is worse.

I park my truck and walk up to Maeve's door. She answers before I knock.

"What is it with my sisters hovering by the front door?"

"You literally just texted four minutes ago and said you were on your way," she reminds me and leads me back to her huge kitchen that looks out to the sea.

We're all ocean-lovers. It's the Irish in us. We come from a small village on the cliffs of Ireland's west coast, and we long for the sea.

"I have a few things to say." I lean on the counter and watch as Maggie shoves a muffin into her mouth. "You're such a lady."

"I know." Her mouth is full when she smiles.

"Why did you tell Izzy that I'm afraid of commitment?"

They look at each other and then both look at their muffins.

"Hungry?" Maggie asks, holding one up for me.

"Answer me, Mary Margaret."

"It wasn't a lie," Maeve says. "You've never been the kind to date anyone for long, Keegan, and that's the truth of it."

"You don't know the reasons behind that. I've never told you that I don't want to meet someone and be with them for the long haul. I've also never said that I broke up with girls, mostly because they were too clingy, or went back to an ex-boyfriend, or thought that owning a pub was beneath them."

"Who was that snobby bitch?" Maggie demands.

"Just because I'm in my mid-thirties and unmarried doesn't make me a confirmed bachelor. And I would hope that before you warn a woman off me, you'd ask me about my intentions."

"You're right," Maeve says, holding up her hand. "We spoke out of turn. But Keegan, Izzy is just so *nice*, and she's been through a lot. We didn't want her to get hurt."

"You may have had her best interests at heart, but

you almost cost me the best thing that's walked into my bar in a long damn time."

"Wait a minute." Maggie stands and walks around the breakfast bar to stand in front of me then narrows her eyes. "You're in love with her."

"I didn't say that."

"You wouldn't be giving us a tongue-lashing if she were just another tumble, Keegan."

"Maeve," I say without answering Maggie, "I need you to cover Izzy's shifts for a couple of days."

"When?"

"Starting today."

"*Today?*"

I nod. "Yeah, sorry for the short notice. Is it not a good fit for you?"

"I can make it work. But I'm so intrigued right now, I don't even know where to begin."

"You can begin by minding your own damn business."

Maggie shakes her head. "I *live* with her."

"That doesn't mean you can't mind yours, Mary Margaret. You didn't act this way with Kane and Shawn. What's gotten into you?"

She blows out a breath and then shrugs as she picks at her muffin. "Maybe I see myself in her. She did what I didn't have the guts to do when I married Joey. I *knew* marrying him was a bad idea, but I didn't have the strength to call it off. She's badass, and I feel a little protective of her."

I immediately soften toward my baby sister. She went through a lot with an abusive husband and then dealing with his death not long ago.

"You're stronger than you give yourself credit for, lass. And it's glad I am that you like her and want her to be safe. I won't intentionally hurt her."

"I know," Maggie says.

"Well, I'm happy for you. Where are you taking her?" Maeve asks.

"Just to the cabin. I want to spend some uninterrupted time with her, and that's hard to do when we're both tied to the pub."

"That's so romantic," Maggie says.

"I'm glad you think so because I need you to run home and pack her a bag. I'm surprising her."

"I can do that. When are you picking her up?"

"As soon as I go check on Ma. Is she upstairs?"

"Oh, no. She and Da went to see Shawn and Lexi today." Maeve smiles.

"Then it looks like I'll be seeing the whole family this morning. How is she feeling?"

"Ma's fine." Maeve takes a bite of her muffin. "She just had a day that her upper back and shoulder were bothering her. But she's fine now."

"It's glad I am to hear it, but I'll go see for myself."

"I'd better get home, then," Maggie says. "I think Izzy went to Target to do some shopping. So, if I'm quick, I'll beat her, and she won't know what hit her."

"Thank you."

"You're welcome. And I'm sorry for almost messing it all up for you. That's not what I meant to do."

"I know. Just don't do it again." I grab two muffins on my way out to the truck. I need to hurry over to check on my parents and ask if Da will take care of the pub for me while I'm gone.

I know he'll jump at the chance, but I still need to ask.

AFTER SPENDING the morning talking with my family and checking on my ma, I'm ready to get out of town for a little vacation.

Words I wouldn't have thought I'd say in the past, but here we are.

When I pull up in front of Maggie's house, Izzy is just stepping out of her sexy little convertible.

"Hey." She grins as I approach and then tips her plump lips up to mine for a kiss.

I happily oblige.

"And hello to you."

"I wasn't expecting to see you until I went into work later." She reaches into the backseat and retrieves several white and red bags. "I just spent *two hours* at Target. You walk in there thinking you need just a handful of things, and the next thing you know, you're crawling down every aisle and tossing things into the basket that you didn't even know you needed. It's true what they say. You don't tell Target what you need. Target tells you."

"All of this sounds ridiculous to me." But she's beautiful today, with her hair pulled back in a low knot on the back of her head, tendrils falling around her sweet face.

She laughs and lets me take some of the bags, then kisses my biceps. "I know. You're a man. You don't understand the Target vortex. What are you up to?"

"I'm here to surprise you."

"That's sweet."

"No, I'm here to really surprise you."

She pushes the front door open and frowns up at me as we walk inside. "What do you mean?"

I glance at Maggie as she walks in with a big grin on her face. "Did you do what I asked?"

"Yep."

"What did you ask?" Izzy demands.

"She packed you a bag. I'm taking you away for a couple of days."

Izzy's eyes light up with excitement, and then she frowns. "But we have work."

"All covered."

"Okay, this is awesome. Where are we going?"

"You'll see when we get there. Do you get car sick?"

She laughs in surprise. "Not usually."

I nod as Maggie wheels the bag in from the kitchen where she had it hidden.

"Oh, let me just grab a few things from these bags."

Izzy rummages through the sacks, consolidates a few, and then smiles at me. "Okay. I'm ready. This is fun."

"Have a good time, and don't worry about a thing," Maggie says. "We've all got the pub under control."

I load Izzy's things into the truck, and it's not long before we're off, headed off the island and north of Seattle.

"I love road trips. Obviously, given that's how I ended up here to begin with."

"I think that was the adrenaline talking."

She nods and stares out the passenger window as the scenery passes us by. "Probably. But my adrenaline knew what it was doing, that's for sure. What prompted you to do this?"

"I think we just need a little time alone. No meddling sisters. No busy and demanding pub."

"You're right. This will be so nice. When was the last time you took a vacation?"

"Last Christmas. I went to Ireland with the whole family for Kane's exhibit debut. That's also when Shawn and Lexi got engaged. It was a great trip. Before that, it had been two years."

"That's a long time without a break. But, honestly, I was the same way. I used to travel all the time when I was a teenager and into college. My mom would drag me all over the world because she didn't like to travel alone."

"Do you like to travel?"

"Sure, I like to see new places. But I've never been to Ireland."

"Well, you might someday."

She grins. "I wouldn't mind that at all. Do you still have a lot of family there?"

"We do, yes. My da's brother's family owns an inn on the sea there. It's a big family. A bit loud. A lot crazy."

"Sounds wonderful."

"They are. Sometimes, they visit the States, but we usually don't see them unless we go there. The inn is beautiful. Fancy, really."

"So, when are we going?"

I laugh and reach over to take her hand in mine, then kiss her knuckles. "Whenever you want, love."

CHAPTER 9

~IZZY~

he drive has been absolutely gorgeous. I
don't know how I've lived in the Pacific
Northwest all my life and never knew how beautiful
the Seattle area is.

I guess my family focused on fancy vacations rather
than taking trips in our own back yard.

"We're about there," Keegan says as he turns onto a
narrow, dirt road that's in surprisingly good condition.
When he rounds a bend and stops in front of a big,
beautiful log cabin with windows to die for, I feel my
jaw drop.

"Whoa." I swallow and look around at the mountains, the trees. "You own this?"

"The family does," he corrects, looking up at it with
me. "Kane fronted most of the money, but the rest of us
pitched in and came out to spend a few weeks offering
up elbow grease to update things. It wasn't in bad

shape to begin with, but it was outdated. So I had the kitchen completely redone."

"Of course." I grin over at him.

"Shawn and Maeve handled remodeling the bedrooms and putting in a gym downstairs, Maggie was in charge of the hot tub out back. Come on. I'll take you on a tour."

"I can't wait." I don't even wait for Keegan to come open my door. I jump out and hurry up the front steps to watch as Keegan keys in a code.

"Welcome to the O'Callaghan cabin," he says as he sweeps the door open and gestures for me to step inside.

"This is seriously amazing." I walk through the foyer to the living room and stare out the floor-to-ceiling windows with an incredible view of the mountains beyond. "Your family has access to the ocean *and* the mountains. That's pretty cool."

"I can't argue with that." He takes my hand and leads me into the open kitchen, all done in white with the biggest island I've ever seen—and I've been inside some incredible homes. This island would make Joanna Gaines weep with joy.

"You designed the kitchen?"

"I helped," he says. "I wanted it to be big enough for our whole growing family to be in here together comfortably. We tend to gather in the kitchen."

"A lot of families do."

"It's particularly fun when Ma is in here cooking up

a storm, and we all sit at the island and pester her. She smiles the whole time. She doesn't really mind."

"Of course, she doesn't. I really like your parents."

He grins and then takes my hand, showing me the butler's pantry, which just happens to be stocked full of my favorite snacks.

"How did this happen?" I gape up at him in shock.

"We have caretakers, and I put a call in." He kisses the top of my head before showing me the hot tub outside, which I hope we put to good use later. He then shows me the beautiful bedrooms—both upstairs and down—a small gym, and a media room.

"There is literally everything you could possibly need up here."

"That was the goal, to be able to escape for a few days with all the comforts of home."

"When you said *cabin*, I thought it would be a bit more rustic."

"That's funny because Lexi had the same response when Shawn first brought her up here. She was convinced they'd be roughing it for a few days."

"I wouldn't mind that," I admit.

"Really?"

"I *loved* summer camp when I was a kid. My favorite nights were the ones when we'd sleep in tents. I like to hike and fish and do all the outdoorsy things."

His hands are on his hips as he stares at me in what looks like shock.

"You don't strike me as the outdoorsy type."

"Why? Because I also like makeup and pretty clothes? I can be a girly-girl and still enjoy a good hike. I just don't get to do it often because my parents thought it was barbaric. They said if I wanted to spend some time outside, they'd send me to a spa where I could sit by the pool."

"It seems to me they just don't understand you at all, love."

I look up at him in surprise. "I guess I never thought of it like that, but you're right. They don't understand me. And I don't think they ever have, honestly."

"Well, we're going to have plenty of time to hike, and if you'd like to fish, we can go over to Shawn's property nearby and fish on his lake. What do you want to do first?"

I tap my chin and look around the big house, and then I grin up at this sexy, sweet man.

"You. I want to do *you* first."

Keegan's green eyes darken, and the next thing I know, he slings me over his shoulder and smacks my ass as he stomps up the stairs to the bedroom we chose as ours for the next few days.

"This is quite caveman of you, you know."

"They would have dragged you by your hair, I'm carrying you."

I giggle and pat his ass in delight before he tosses me onto the soft, luxurious bed.

"Shawn and Maeve did a good job in these bedrooms. The bed is to die for."

"You haven't seen anything yet, lass."

Keegan's still sleeping when I slip out of bed and walk into the en suite bathroom. We never left the house to enjoy the great outdoors last night. We spent the whole time in bed, making love and talking. Laughing. Then we raided the kitchen for sustenance before starting all over again.

It's the most fun I've ever had with a man in my whole life.

Is it sad that I'm on the downslope to thirty and didn't know that being with a man could be so *fun*? So good for me?

I turn on the spray in the walk-in shower that's big enough for a party of four, and as it heats up, I comb out my hair and gather my shampoo, conditioner, and body wash, finally stepping inside the delectable spray.

I'm no stranger to beautiful homes. My parents are wealthy, and their home is full of grandeur, bordering on pompous. Obnoxious, even. They're all about showing off their wealth, rather than using it for comfort.

That's not what this house is. Yes, it's absolutely beautiful, with all of the finest furnishings money can buy. But it's all been done so the family is comfortable. While absolutely lovely, I'm not afraid to *live* here. To put my feet on an ottoman or hop up onto the kitchen counter and watch as Keegan whips up an omelet. This home was designed with enjoyment in mind.

I've been here for less than twenty-four hours, and I'm more comfortable than I ever was in the many years I lived with my parents.

And I know, deep down, that if I'd married Troy, the same would have been true there. He intended to build a monstrosity of a house to show off to others, not for our comfort.

That would have sucked.

I just finished rinsing the conditioner out of my hair when I feel Keegan join me. He wraps his arms around my waist from behind and kisses the side of my neck.

"Good morning," he growls.

"Good morning." I feel him pressed against my back, already hard and ready to go.

Or maybe it's just morning, and he's simply hard.

"You left me."

I laugh and turn in his arms. His eyes are still heavy with sleep. "I woke up and found I needed a hot shower to soothe my muscles after yesterday's sexcapades."

"We can sit in the hot tub for that."

"We tried that last night, and it only led to more sexcapades."

He laughs and reaches for the soap. "You didn't seem to mind."

"Oh, I'm definitely not complaining." He lathers up his hands and gets to work running them all over my body, starting with my shoulders. In the past, I would have been mortified at the thought of standing naked in front of a man in the shower.

But not with Keegan. He's made it perfectly clear that he *loves* my body, from my bigger-than-I'd-prefer breasts to my curvy hips and thighs that have a touch of cellulite. None of it bothers him at all. In fact, when he touches me, it's as if he *worships* me.

And it almost gives me a high.

Every woman should be treated this way.

Maybe I should take out an ad somewhere to let the others know.

I smirk when his thumb brushes over my nipple, making him raise a brow.

"Is that funny, lass?"

I press my lips together and shake my head. "Sorry, I was just thinking."

"And what's on your mind?"

"It's dumb. Please continue."

He kisses my forehead as his hands travel down my belly and over my thighs.

Nothing about this is funny. It's sexy as hell.

And yet, I still have the giggles from a second ago. I hold my breath, trying to keep it in.

But I can't.

I snort just as his fingers glide down my ass crack.

"Not the reaction I expected."

"I'm sorry." I tip my forehead to his chest and give in to the giggles. "I was just thinking—"

But I can't continue as laughter bubbles out of me. It's not even that funny. But this is one of those moments in life when the stupid giggles set in, and they won't stop. You just have to ride the wave until they subside.

When I pull back, I see Keegan grinning down at me. He rinses his hands free of soap and wipes the tears off my cheeks.

"I need to be let in on the joke."

"It's so dumb." I take a deep breath and then giggle again when I hiccup. "I'm embarrassed to tell you now because it's not funny, and you'll be let down."

He patiently rinses the soap off my body. The man makes me swoon.

When I'm clean, he shuts off the water and reaches for the towels.

"I'm sorry, I ruined the mood."

He turns to me quickly and pulls me into his arms. "You didn't ruin anything at all. We're having fun together, and that's all that matters. We can christen the shower later."

"You're a good man, you know that, right?"

"I do okay." He winks and wraps me in the towel. "Tell me what made you laugh. If you say it was my attempt at seduction, you'll wound me deeply."

I let out a snort laugh. "No. It definitely wasn't that. I was just thinking that before I knew you, I didn't know that being with a man could be so *fun* and easy and good for me. And that I should probably take out an ad somewhere to tell others."

"*Others?*"

"Yeah. You know, other women who have put up with less-than-stellar men because they think that's as good as it gets. Someone needs to clue them in that it can be so much better."

"That isn't a bad idea," he says as he slips his T-shirt over his head and tosses me the clothes I brought with me into the bathroom. "*What every woman in an average relationship needs to know.*"

"Yes! And I don't know why it made me giggle. But it did. And then I just couldn't stop."

Now that we're dressed in our comfy clothes, he crosses to me and frames my face in his hands. "It's glad I am that this isn't average for you."

"Definitely not average. Not at all."

A smile tickles his lips before they descend on mine. He takes his time, kissing me long and slow before pulling away.

"We need food," he says.

"I can cook breakfast."

"I didn't know you could cook."

"You never asked." I toss him a sassy smile and lead him out of the bedroom suite and down to the kitchen. "You just sit there and look handsome while I pull this together."

He rests his chin in his hand as I bustle about,

retrieving a pan and the ingredients for a classic American breakfast.

I'm pleased to find frozen hash browns in the freezer, fresh eggs, bacon, and bread for toast.

"How do you like your eggs?" I ask.

"Whatever's easiest for you is fine."

I raise a brow. "How do you prefer them?"

"Over-medium."

I nod once and get to work. It's not a time-consuming meal, you just have to keep an eye on things so you don't overcook anything. Timing is everything.

Before long, I've plated his meal and slide it over to him.

He takes a bite of the perfectly crisp bacon, then stares at me as if I hung the moon.

"It's just bacon, Keegan."

"I should have you in the kitchen, not the bloody bar."

"Don't you dare take me out of the bar." I take a bite of my breakfast. "I like it too much. The regular customers are fun, and I'm just now getting the hang of it."

"I can't keep anyone in the kitchen," he admits. "That's why Shawn and Lexi are in there so much. I had a part-time helper, but he moved to Seattle to be with his girlfriend. I need more staff."

I watch as he works his way through his plate. "Do you have a high turnover for any specific reason?"

"The kitchen can be demanding," he admits. "We

have a good-sized menu, and when it's busy, it's *busy*. I've never had another bartender because I'm usually there. If Da's in town, he'll cover if need be. Shawn or Maeve can help in a pinch. If I'm gone for more than a day or two, I shut the bar down."

I frown at him. "That's a lot of pressure on you, Keegan."

"I own the pub."

"Yes, you do. Which is why you need to hire employees you trust to help you. Bartend every day if you want to, but you shouldn't have to close down just because you're taking a holiday."

He sighs as he finishes his plate. "I've given some thought to bringing in more help. I'll think on it more."

"I suspect you think about things until you drive yourself crazy."

"Sometimes." He stands and carries his plate to the sink, then leans over and kisses my cheek. "Thank you for this delicious breakfast."

"You're welcome."

"Would you like to join me on a hike?"

"Hell, yes.

"This is incredible." I prop my hands on my hips as I try to catch my breath. We just made it to the top of a trail that led us to the top of a hill that offers the most beautiful view I've ever seen. "I can even see the house from here."

He nods and rests his foot on a boulder and leans on his knee. "When Kane and I came up here to check out the property, we found this trail and followed it up here. As soon as we stood here and saw the view, we knew we had to buy it."

"You and Kane are close."

"We're only a year apart in age," Keegan says. "He was my first friend and still is my best friend. He's always been the more serious one, the artistic one. When we were small and still in Ireland, before our parents came to the US, he loved to spend hours upon hours in our uncle's barn, firing glass."

"It's fascinating to me. I've never seen how glass is made."

"I'm pretty sure we could show you how it's done, if you're interested."

"I would have to be an idiot to turn down the chance to watch Kane O'Callaghan at work."

"You've heard of him, then?"

"Of course. I've seen his work before. It's all over the world."

"We're all damn proud of him."

"I think you're all worth being proud of."

He laces his fingers with mine and raises my hand to his lips. "Let's get back to the house so I can get you naked and pick up where we left off in the shower this morning."

"Not a bad idea at all. Let's go."

We hustle down the trail and make it back to the trailhead in half the time it took us to hike up. Just as we walk into the house, we hear Keegan's phone ringing, but then it stops.

"You just missed a call."

He shrugs but reaches for his cell. We left both devices sitting on the kitchen counter when we took off for our hike.

Keegan scowls. "Christ Jesus, the family's been blowing it up."

I glance at mine and see I've missed several calls from Maggie, as well.

"My mother hasn't felt well." His face is lined with worry as he dials and puts the phone to his ear. "What's going on, Maeve?"

He listens, and then his eyes narrow as he looks over at me. "Are they okay? How soon? Well, she doesn't waste any time, does she? We'll wrap things up here and head back. No, we should be there. We own the bloody place, Maeve, we'll be back. See you soon."

"Is your mom okay?"

"It's Anastasia." He sighs and looks at me with regret. "I'm sorry, love, but we'll have to cut our trip short. The baby's on its way, and it seems he or she wants to make a dramatic entrance. Stasia's having some complications. Kane's beside himself."

"We need to get there," I say immediately and hurry for the stairs. "I can be packed in five minutes."

"Stop."

I turn to find him just behind me. He drags his knuckles down my cheek.

"What is it?"

"Thank you."

"For not being a bitch because your brother is about to be a father?"

He smiles. "Something like that."

"You're welcome. Now let's get a move on."

CHAPTER 10

"You can go up without me. I'm not trying to keep you from them, I just have to get a gift before I go in there."

I grin down at her as she fusses over some pink and blue blankets in the hospital gift shop.

"I can wait ten more minutes."

"I just don't know if I should get something for the baby or for Anastasia."

"We can get something for both of them," I suggest. "Get all of it, if you want."

She sighs and bites her lower lip, concentrating way harder than I think is necessary, but I'm not a woman. They're a mystery to me.

"Wait." She turns to me with wide eyes. "Do we know if it's a boy or a girl?"

"No, because we aren't upstairs yet."

"Well, crap." She finally decides on a yellow giraffe

blanket and a bigger, fluffier gray blanket for Stasia. "Okay, I'll start here and shop for more later."

"All right, let's do this."

I pay for the gifts, along with the gift bags to stuff them in for exactly six minutes, and earn a glare from Izzy.

"What?"

"I was supposed to buy them."

"Can't they be from us?"

"Oh, of course. I just didn't want to assume that would be okay."

I stop us in the hospital hallway and turn her to me. I tip up her chin. "You and I are an *us*, Isabella. I didn't realize that wasn't already implied, so I'm happy to make it clear right here and now."

Her lips tip up into a grin. "Well, okay then. Let's go meet a baby."

I kiss her lips before taking her hand and leading her into an elevator and up to the labor and delivery part of the hospital.

It's been a few hours since that call to Maeve at the cabin. From what I understand, Stasia has since had an emergency C-section, and both she and the baby are safe.

But they don't want to tell me what the sex is until we get there.

"What room is she in?" Izzy asks.

"That one at the end of the hall."

"How do you know?"

I grin at the laughter and chatter coming from the room. "Because I can hear them. We're not a quiet lot, that's for sure."

Izzy and I fill the doorway, and I smile at the scene before me.

Anastasia is sitting up in the hospital bed, wearing a tired smile and an IV in one arm. Kane sits close by, one hand on her ankle as he talks with Anastasia's brother, Archer, and his wife, Elena.

My mother rocks the new baby in the corner as my father stands next to her and smiles down at the wee one.

Maggie and Maeve are on their phones, most likely methodically calling all of the Montgomerys and O'Callaghans all over the bloody world.

"You're here," Stasia says. "Come in."

"Is there room?" I ask, teasing her. "You're awfully popular."

I walk to her and kiss her cheek before circling the bed to hug my brother.

"Shawn and Lexi just left," he says. "Amelia and Wyatt are on their way."

"What about your parents?" I ask Stasia.

"They just went down to the cafeteria for some lunch."

"So, it's been a revolving door."

"I just got off the phone with Will," Maeve adds. "He and Meg will be here this evening. He can't get out of practice since they have a game in a few days."

I glance back at Izzy, who's still hovering in the doorway.

"Come in, love. We don't bite."

"I should wait in the waiting room. I don't want to overwhelm—"

"If you don't get in here," Anastasia says, "I'll be offended."

Izzy laughs and steps inside, then offers Stasia the gift bags. "We stopped downstairs to get a little something."

"Oh, you didn't have to...thank God, blankets! Everything happened so fast this morning, I forgot to bring the baby's blankets and one for me. I'm always cold. This is absolutely perfect, Izzy, thank you."

"You're welcome."

"Izzy, this is my brother, Archer. You met his wife, Elena, at the baby shower."

"Nice to meet you."

"Hey, why did Archer get out of going to the baby shower?" I ask.

"I had work," the other man says with a smug grin.

"Is anyone going to tell us if it's a boy or a girl?" Izzy asks the room.

"It's a boy," Kane says proudly. "Thomas Edward O'Callaghan."

Named for our father, and for Anastasia's. "That's a fine name if ever I heard one."

"Come." My mother gestures to Izzy. "Give him a cuddle."

"Oh, Keegan should hold him first."

I shake my head. "You go ahead. Really."

Izzy doesn't so much as look my way as my mother gently lays the baby in Izzy's arms and then gestures for her to sit in the rocking chair.

The baby doesn't even make a peep as Izzy slowly rocks back and forth and gazes down at him as if in awe.

"Well, aren't you a tiny one?" She drags her finger down his little cheek. "You'd make a woman's ovaries explode."

We all laugh, and the girls nod in agreement.

"He's the sweetest baby," Ma says. "Just content to sleep away."

"He's already eaten, too," Stasia adds.

"Yes, you're a healthy little fella," Izzy coos and pushes his hat back so she can see his hair. "And you have your daddy's dark hair. You're already a heartbreaker."

"What happened this morning?" I ask as Izzy rocks the baby.

"My water broke, and everything seemed fine, but when we got here, they said he was turned awkwardly, and I'd never be able to push him out. So, they had to rush us back for surgery."

"Thank goodness you're both safe now," Maggie says.

"Okay, it's your turn." Izzy turns to me, but I shake my head.

I'm terrified of him.

"I think I'll wait until he's not so fragile." But I squat next to them and rub his small fingers. He wraps his hand around my finger, and that's all it takes to send me head over heels in love with him. "Well, hello there, sweet Tommy. I'm your uncle Keegan. I'll be your favorite."

I hear laughter around me, and when I glance up, I find my mother smiling softly down at me.

I know what she's thinking.

And for the first time in my life, I'd say she's not wrong.

"Okay, stop hogging the baby," Maeve says as she approaches. "I've only held him for a second, and then I had to call everyone in the world."

"Go snuggle your auntie Maeve," Izzy singsongs before kissing his little forehead, which wrinkles at her touch. "Oh, my goodness, I love it when babies wrinkle their tiny brows like that."

"I just want to eat him up," Maeve says as she gently takes him from Izzy.

"You baked a beautiful baby," I say to Stasia. She smiles, but her eyes are droopy. "And now we're going to leave you be so you can rest."

"You don't have to go," she insists, but I see the fatigue, and I don't want to overwhelm her.

"We'll be back," I assure her. I step to my brother and bring him in for another hug. "Congratulations, Kane."

"Thank you." He smiles. "He's something, isn't he?"

"He's the best. Going to be pampered and loved more than anyone I know."

He grins. "As it should be. I'll see you later?"

"You couldn't keep us away. I think Izzy might be obsessed."

"It's a *baby*," she says. "Of course, I'm obsessed."

We say our goodbyes and head out of the room.

"He's *adorable*." Izzy grins. "And so tiny."

"I take it you like babies, then?"

"What's not to like? I would say I'm a maternal person. I always begged for a baby brother or sister, but my mom wouldn't do it. Now, I need to get home so I can cook."

"What are you cooking, love?"

"I need to make some meals for them. She just had major abdominal surgery, Keegan, she can't be cooking."

I want to pull her to me and kiss the hell out of her. I want to propose to her, right here and now.

Jesus, I have it bad.

"I think my ma will have the meals down. Well, her, along with Stasia's family."

"Oh. You're right. I wasn't thinking. But I want to do *something* for them. I'm so excited. Then again, it's not really my place to butt in and do anything at all, of course. I'm being silly."

"You're being sweet, and there's nothing wrong with that at all, Isabella. If you'd like to help out, I'm sure there's plenty they'll need. Everyone will want to jump in and help this week. But after the newness wears off, they'll still need some help. Maybe we can do something then?"

"That's a good idea." She smiles as we exit the hospital and walk toward the truck. "What now?"

"Well, we were supposed to spend the day in bed, but we got a little sidetracked."

"I'm hungry," she announces. "Feed me, and then bed."

"I can work with that."

"I LEFT my lucky lipstick up in your apartment," Izzy announces as she hurries into the bar. It's been a few days since wee Thomas was born, and we've gone back to our usual routine of work, sex, and enjoying each other.

I can't say that it's a bad life we're living.

"You can go on up and fetch it, then," I say, but she's already gone, clomping up the steps to the flat above. When she returns, she's in no less of a hurry. "What are you all dressed up for?"

"Oh, I'm doing my audition videos today." She smooths the lipstick on her lips and rubs them together. "Your sisters are helping me."

"What audition videos?"

She blinks up at me. "I didn't tell you?"

"No. You didn't."

"I'm sorry, I must have forgotten. Maeve and Maggie talked me into applying for some meteorologist jobs at networks, and part of the application packet is a video of me reporting the weather."

"That's wonderful. I hope it's Seattle that you're applying for."

She checks the time. "Of course, Seattle. Okay, gotta run."

"Don't be so nervous. You're going to be great."

She takes a deep breath and grins at me. "Thank you. I needed that. I'll see you in a few hours."

I wave her off, and just as she opens the door, she almost runs right into Archer.

"Excuse me, Archer."

"My fault," he replies and holds the door for her, then wanders into the pub. "Where's the fire?"

I laugh and wipe down the bar with my rag. "She's meeting up with my sisters this afternoon. What are you doing on the island today, Archer?"

"I came over to see my sister and the baby." He sits on a stool and leans on his forearms. "Thought I'd stop in and see how you're doing."

"I'm doing better than I have in a long while. Are you here to get drunk again?"

Archer laughs and then shakes his head. "Hell, no, that was a one-night deal."

"How's Elena?"

His face lights up at the mention of his new bride.

Archer and Elena were high school sweethearts and recently reconnected and married.

I can see by the look on his face that things are going well.

"She's beautiful. Amazing. Perfect."

"So fine, then, I take it."

He chuckles and then nods. "You could say that, yes. I'm still getting used to her crazy family, but we all have crazy families, right?"

"I can't say that we're all married into the mafia," I say thoughtfully. "But there is a level of insanity in all families, yes."

"Well, so far, everything has been good. Now, enough about me." He gestures with his thumb toward the front door. "She seems nice. Elena said she enjoyed her a lot at Stasia's shower."

"Izzy's nice, yes."

The other man's eyes narrow. "Cut the bullshit with me, Keegan. We're better friends than that."

"She's beautiful. Amazing. Perfect."

He nods in satisfaction. "That's what I thought. And when are you going to marry her?"

My hand stops moving on the bar, and I stare at him as if he's crazy. "I've known her for seven minutes, Archer."

"You and I are similar men. We're not the kind to fuck around with women just for the sake of fucking around. Not at this stage in our lives. I see the way you look at Izzy. What does it matter if

137

you've known her for seven minutes or seven years?"

"She has a past."

"We all do."

"I think we're both content with where we're at for now."

"And where are you, exactly?"

"Mutual admiration, lust, and still learning each other."

He nods and raps his knuckles on the bar. "That's not a bad place to be. For what it's worth, the family likes her. The little bit I've heard has all been good."

"It's worth a lot. You know how much the family means to me."

"Yeah, I do."

"How is the baby today?"

"The most adorable thing I've ever seen in my life." He grins. "Your brother is completely enamored with both of them. He has a goofy smile on his face and dotes like a little old lady. It's hilarious to watch."

"I can honestly say I never thought I'd see the day that Kane would become a family man. He's so fucking grouchy, I didn't think anyone would put up with him for long."

Archer laughs and nods in agreement. "But Stasia puts him in his place easily enough."

"And only she can. I love her like my own sisters."

"I know you do. She's easy to love. I'm glad they brought our families together."

"Me, too. Are you sure I can't interest you in a pint?"

"Nah. I have to head back. I'm looking at some properties today, and I promised Elena I'd take her out to her favorite place for dinner. But I'm sure I'll see you soon."

"I look forward to it."

IT'S the busiest Friday night we've had in a long time, even with it being the shoulder season—the time between the tourism highs and lows. I called in Maeve to help Maggie and Izzy buzz around the pub, taking and delivering orders.

The band is lively and barely covers the sound of the patrons, all laughing and talking.

It's a sight that reminds me of the pub in our little village in Ireland. The sights and sounds, and even the scents coming from the kitchen, are the same.

I've been homesick more and more over the past few months, which is unlike me.

It seems a lot is changing in me lately.

"I need four pints of Guinness and a shot of whiskey," Maeve says as she sets her empty tray on the bar. "And I might need a security guard in a minute."

"Who's bothering you?"

My eyes narrow as I scan my pub.

"Far back right corner." She jerks her chin and rolls

her eyes. "They're good and pissed and think it's okay to put their hands where they're not wanted."

"Cut them off now and tell them to leave."

"It's been pretty harmless until my last trip over."

"We have no tolerance for this, Maeve. I'll escort them out if you'd rather."

She blows out a breath and shakes her head, her red hair swishing in its ponytail. "No, I'll tell them."

She loads up her drinks and delivers them to a nearby table before making her way to the back corner. I keep watch to make sure the men leave quietly.

Maeve smiles as she gestures to the door.

Two of the men's faces sober, and they look at the other two, who scowl. The biggest one stands.

And gets in my sister's face.

I hurry around the bar, and just as I reach them, Maeve pours a drink over the man's head.

"That should cool you off, you misogynistic ass," she says. "Now, take your goons and get the hell out of my pub."

"Maybe someone needs to teach you your fucking place," the man growls, but I step up and move Maeve behind me.

"Why don't you teach *me*?"

I tower over the piece of shit by at least six inches. He looks up and swallows hard. "This isn't any of your fucking business."

"As I'm the owner here, and this is my sister, it's

absolutely my business. She asked you to leave. You won't be asked nicely again."

"Are you gonna try to throw us out of here? There's four of us, asshole."

"And there's four of us," Will Montgomery says from behind me. I glance back to see that he has his brothers, Matt and Caleb, with him.

The four of us look formidable, and the four of *them* swallow hard in response.

"That's Will Montgomery," one of them observes.

"And he's going to kick your ass if you don't fucking *leave*," Will says.

They scoot out of the booth and hurry out of the bar, and then the band picks back up, and everyone goes back to their drinks.

Squabbles aren't unheard of in an Irish pub.

"What are you all doing here?" I ask as I turn to shake their hands. "Wait, let me guess. You went to see the baby."

"We did," Matt agrees. "We had some time and decided to come to the island for a few hours."

"The girls are going to be pissed that we didn't bring them," Caleb adds, but then shrugs. "They thought we were just having a boring guys' night."

"We'll bring them back in a couple of days," Will says, unconcerned. "I've always wanted to swing in here and see what it's like. It's damn awesome, Keegan."

"That it is. Let me pour you each a pint."

"I'll take a Coke," Matt interrupts. "I'll drive these two home."

"Deal," Caleb agrees, and the three of them sit at the bar.

Izzy's been in and out of the kitchen and didn't miss a step seeing to her tables during the exchange with the assholes. She grins and waves at the guys as she hurries into the kitchen.

"I'm hungry," Will says. "I'll take everything on the appetizer menu."

"We're going to be here all fucking night." Caleb groans.

"I'm *hungry*," Will repeats.

"Okay, make it two," Caleb says.

"I'll just eat some of theirs," Matt adds but earns glares from his brothers. "Fine, I'll have the nachos. And the wings. And bring some fries, too."

"Three orders of the appetizer menu, it is."

CHAPTER 11

"Fucking Christ, you'll end up killing me," Keegan pants, his weight on me, still inside of me. This is the very best way to wake up every morning.

I don't remember the last time I slept at Maggie's house. The thought of being away from Keegan at night isn't one I want to entertain.

It's just too good to be with him. To feel him next to me.

To wake up to *this.*

I drag my fingers up and down his back, and he kisses my cheek before rolling to the side.

"Good morning." I kiss his chin.

"And a good morning to you." He drags his hand through his dark, messy hair. "I need to shave this morning."

"I like the scruff." I rub the tip of my nose over the stubble on his chin. "It's sexy."

"There will be no more shaving, ever again, by order of the queen."

I laugh and shake my head at him. "Well, we don't want you to look like Santa or anything."

"You have something against beards, then?"

"No." I let my eyes roam over his face, taking him in. "You'd look good with a short beard. Just don't let it go and get dirty and full of food and stuff."

"That's disgusting." He swats my ass playfully and then rolls away. "Let's get in the shower."

"I'm spent." I pull the covers up over my nakedness. "I can't do shower sex right now, Keegan, no matter how fun it sounds."

He laughs again and reaches for my hand. "It's not my intention to ravage you in the shower. We'll save that for another day. But I'm hungry, and I need to clean up before I can take you out to breakfast."

"Well, why didn't you say so?" I climb out of bed and hurry to the bathroom, where Keegan starts the water.

He takes his time washing my hair, rubbing my scalp so thoroughly that I swear I could fall asleep standing up.

Once I'm rinsed, I help him wash up, then we climb out and dry off.

"Getting ready in the morning goes fast when I don't have to shave," he says with a grin as he slips a black T-shirt over his head and reaches for his jeans. His eyes haven't left me as I get dressed in denim shorts and a loose tank top.

"What is it?" I ask.

"You're so fucking beautiful, I can hardly stand it, Isabella."

Those words coming from any man have the power to make a woman smile. Coming from *this* man, in that incredible accent, it melts my insides.

"Thank you."

"Why do you get flustered when I compliment you?"

"Because it's unexpected and hot as hell, honestly."

With a cocky grin, he steps to me and plants those magical lips on mine for a long, slow kiss. "Let's go eat."

"Good idea."

But when we're in the truck headed into town, he doesn't park in front of the diner.

"No oatmeal this morning?"

"This is a date," he says. "I'm taking you somewhere new. Well, new to you. There's a deli just around the corner here that has good breakfast."

He helps me out of the truck and then holds the door of the deli. Once inside, we order breakfast burritos and sit in the corner to eat.

One bite in, and I know this is *not* as good as the diner.

Keegan and I look up at each other.

"So, should we go to the diner for oatmeal?" I ask.

"Yeah. We should." We stand and take the burritos with us, and Keegan stashes them in the backseat of his truck. "I don't want to throw them away. Shawn's the one who said this place was great. I'll see if he wants them."

"Good idea."

Before he can pull away from the deli, my phone rings.

"It's my dad," I say in surprise. Keegan puts the truck back in park, and I answer. "Hello?"

"Hello, Izzy. It's your father."

I roll my eyes. "Yes, I have your number programmed, Dad."

"I'll get right to the point of this call. I want to know when you'll be coming home. It's past time you do so."

I sigh and shake my head. "I'm not coming home to live, Dad. I'll come visit if you and Mom want me to, but I won't be living in Salem again."

"This is ridiculous," he mutters on the other end. "You have responsibilities here, young lady. I expect you to take over my company someday."

"No, you expect me to marry someone to take over your company one day, Dad. Because I'm just a woman, and running a multi-million-dollar enterprise isn't appropriate. But I can tell you right now, that's never going to happen."

"Troy is *not* the bad man you've made him out to be," he insists. "In fact, he's a good man, and you need to come here and apologize to him. You need to make things right with him and do your duty to our family."

I sit up straight and stare at my phone. He's lost his damn mind. "I don't think you heard me. I won't apologize to Troy, today or any day. I'm *not* marrying him. If you love him so much, *you* marry him, Dad."

"I didn't raise you to speak to me that way."

"You didn't raise me at all!" I laugh at the absurdity of it. "Nannies raised me. And this is who I am."

"What? A lowly barmaid who barely makes minimum wage in some bumpkin town in Washington?"

"I'm an independent, hardworking, good person in a lovely small community in Washington. You can take it or leave it."

"I'm incredibly disappointed in you, Isabella Marie."

"Likewise. I can tell by your tone that you're going to leave it. And that's fine. You have my number if you need me, but don't use it if you're only going to hound me about marrying an abusive, cheating man just because it fits your needs. Goodbye."

I hang up and toss my phone into my purse.

"I'm so sorry, love."

"I'm not." I shake my head and turn to Keegan. "I'm not sorry at all. It's way past time I stood up to that man. Speak up for myself. He can't bully me into doing what he wants anymore, and it's driving him crazy. But I don't care. He'll learn to live with it. I'm not going back there. I love my life here."

"Good." He leans over to kiss my lips. "It's glad I am that you're happy here."

"I'll be happier if you get your oatmeal."

"On our way." He pulls away from the deli and circles the block to park in front of the diner. "Are you having oatmeal, as well?"

"Hell no, I'm having pancakes."

HOW DARE my father insult my job? I freaking *love* working at the pub. And tonight is no different. It's Saturday night, so we're busy. The band plays on the stage, and Maggie, Maeve, and I work the tables while Keegan and Tom pull the taps, and Fiona, Lexi, and Shawn man the kitchen.

All hands on deck tonight, and I am having the time of my life.

"It's a beauty you are, Miss Izzy," Frank, one of our regulars, says as I set his drink in front of him. His grin widens when I add the burger and fries he ordered. "Run off and marry me, why don't you?"

"Ah, Frank." I pat him on the shoulder and offer him a wink. "You'd be sick of me within a week."

"I beg to differ."

He laughs as I kiss his cheek and then saunter away to put a drink order in with Keegan.

"Flirting with the customers are you, love?" he asks.

"Frank's convinced that I own his heart and proposed for the fourth time this week."

Keegan laughs as Maeve approaches the bar. "He proposed to me just a half-hour ago."

"It's a fickle heart he has, our Frank." Keegan pulls the tap for the Guinness. "How's it going out there, ladies?"

"Fine for me tonight," Maeve says.

"Me, too. It's busy, but everyone seems happy tonight. And with all of us here, it's been smooth sailing."

"That's what we like to hear." Tom winks as he joins Keegan at the taps. "And hello to you, Cameron."

I turn to see Cameron sitting on a stool at the bar. He grins at everyone and nods when Keegan offers him a pint.

"What are you up to this evening?" I ask him.

"Enjoying my last night in town for a couple of weeks."

"You're leaving again, then?" Maggie asks as she takes Maeve's place at the bar. "That sounds about right."

Cameron's blue eyes narrow on Maggie. "You know I always come back."

"It's none of my business, is it?" She turns to Keegan. "I need three pints of Guinness, and I have to go to the kitchen."

She hurries away and leaves Cameron looking after her.

"Why is she so angry with you?" I ask him.

"She hasn't said?"

"No, she doesn't talk about it."

He sighs and looks back toward the kitchen again. A muscle twitches in his jaw as he clenches it shut. "I guess I shouldn't talk about it either, then."

"Well, do something to fix it because neither of you is going anywhere, and Maggie being mad at you forever doesn't sound fun to me."

"It doesn't sound fun to me either," he says. "And I'm working on fixing it. You're bossy, you know that, Izzy?"

I laugh and take my now-full tray off the bar. "Yeah. I know. Here I go."

I make my rounds and drop off drinks. I've just wiped off an empty table when two more men sit down at it.

"Hey, guys, what can I get for you?"

"Just a couple of beers," one of them says. When I glance up, I recognize him right away, but I just smile, take the order, and then walk back to the bar. "Keegan?"

"Yes, love?"

"Aren't those two guys at that table the ones you tossed out of here last night?"

His green eyes narrow as he scans the bar. "They are. I'll tell them to leave."

"Well, they're polite for now. I'll keep an eye on them. Maybe last night was just a bad one."

Keegan presses his lips together. "If they say or do even *one* thing that makes you uncomfortable, you come tell me, and I'll get them out of here."

"I can do that."

I go about the business of delivering food and drinks and talking with the patrons. The evening goes well, and even the two horrible patrons from last night are polite and friendly.

"Hey, we're sorry about last night," the blond one says. "We were just a little too drunk."

"Yeah," the dark-haired one adds. "We didn't mean to be assholes. I'm Larry, and this is Scott."

"It's all good, Larry and Scott. Your food should be up. I'll be back."

They nod as I hurry away. Sure enough, their food is ready. Keegan catches my eye as I make my way back through the bar, but I nod as if to reassure him that everything is fine.

He raises his chin in return.

We've gotten really good at non-verbal communication.

"Okay, guys, I have an order of wings with fries, and a burger with fries hot out of the kitchen." I pull ketchup and mustard out of my apron and set them on the table, as well. "What else can I get you?"

"Your phone number." Scott winks.

"Haha. What can I get you from the kitchen?"

"This looks good," Larry says, and the boys dig into their food.

When I walk up to the bar, Keegan gestures to them. "Everything still good there?"

"Yep, just normal flirtation. And they apologized for last night."

"Good." He wipes the bar and sends me a heated look. "It's easy to flirt with you. You look damn good tonight, love."

I toss my ponytail over my shoulder. "So nice of you to notice."

He laughs, and I saunter away with an extra spring in my step. I stop at Larry and Scott's table to check in with them.

"How's it tasting over here?"

"Great," Scott says, and I notice his eyes drop to my boobs. "I bet those taste good, too."

Larry scoffs at his friend. "Good one, man."

"Don't ruin this," I say. "You'll just piss everyone off again and get thrown out. There's no need for that."

Scott rolls his eyes, and I turn to leave, but suddenly, he grabs my wrist and tugs me onto his lap.

"Hey!"

"I didn't say you could walk away from me." His hand gropes my breast, his beer-laden breath hot on my cheek as he says, "I'm paying you to be *nice* to me, you stupid bitch."

"Fuck y—"

Strong arms pull me out of the asshole's lap. I glance up to see Cameron, his steely blue eyes hard on

Scott as Keegan grabs the man by his shirt and yanks him out of the chair.

"Outside, you piece of rubbish," Keegan growls and hurries out the front door as Scott flails about and yells for Larry.

Cameron and I, along with Maeve and Maggie, hurry after them. Just as I round the corner of the building, I see Keegan bury his fist in Scott's face.

"You think it's okay to touch women like that?" He hits him again.

"Fuck you," Scott growls.

"You're probably a fucking rapist." Keegan plants his knee in Scott's stomach.

"She asked for it," Scott wheezes.

"Someone needs to teach you a goddamn lesson." Again, Keegan's fist connects with Scott's face. Over and over, until blood runs from his nose and trickles from the side of his mouth.

I look up at Cameron. "Aren't you going to stop this?"

"Hell, no, that prick deserves it."

I don't know if I should feel scared, amused, or turned on.

"I'm going to fucking sue you, asshole," Scott says.

"Do it." Keegan's nose is millimeters from Scott's. "Fucking do it. I bet you have sexual assault charges the length of my arm against you, you wanker. And where's your friend now?"

We all look around, and I see Larry walking quickly down the street. He jumps in a car and zooms away.

"He just left," I call out.

"If you *ever* touch any woman like that again, I'll be there, and you'll get it worse than this. If you *ever* make her or anyone else uncomfortable again, I'll fucking kill you. Do you understand me?"

"Fuck you."

"Jesus, man, just stop the macho bullshit," Cameron warns him. "In case you missed it, you lost."

"I'll rape her, and then I'll fuck her pretty little mouth," Scott says.

Keegan rears back and plants his elbow square in the middle of Scott's face, knocking the other man out. He lets him fall to the ground.

"Should I call an ambulance?" Maeve asks.

"No," Keegan replies.

"Probably," Cameron counters.

As he walks over to me, I see that his knuckles are bleeding. "Are you okay?"

"Me? I'm fine. You're the one bleeding. Jesus, Keegan."

"He thought he could touch what's mine, and I assured him that wasn't the case."

Holy hell. "Yes, you did."

The last words Scott said sit in my brain like acid. How can people think that saying shit like that is okay?

"Did he think he sounded badass talking that way?"

I wonder aloud as we file back inside. "Like, are there girls out there who would find that sexy?"

"He doesn't care what they think," Cameron says. "He doesn't respect women at all. Or anyone, really."

Maeve walks in behind us, putting away her phone. "I called an ambulance for him, but I'll be damned if I wait out there. I hope you didn't kill him, Keegan."

"I didn't," he insists as he presses a towel filled with ice against his knuckles. "I know where I'm hitting."

"Do you think he'll really sue you?" I ask.

"I don't fucking care if he does," Keegan says and then reaches out to drag his fingers down my cheek. "When I saw his hands on you, and you fighting to get away, I saw red."

"I guess so. Let's finish work and talk about it later."

I can see that he wants to pull me to him, and I know that we'll have to talk this through later. I can't have Keegan beating up every man who says something inappropriate.

But Scott took it way past inappropriate and into assault.

And that's what I tell the cops when they arrive with the ambulance.

"And you have witnesses?" the cop asks.

"I have a bar full," I assure him. "He was awful, and once outside, threatened to rape me."

He sighs. "He's had other complaints filed against him. When the hospital's done with him, I'll book him —if you want to press charges."

"Yes." I raise my chin and look him in the eyes. "I want to press all the charges. He can't do this to anyone else."

"Good." The cop smiles. "Very good."

When I return to work, the pep has left my step, and the adrenaline is gone, leaving me a little shaky and a lot tired. But I'll be damned if I let another man like Troy or Scott ruin my day or make me run away and hide.

I'm a bit more careful in my flirtation with the customers, and I certainly don't touch anyone in greeting. But I paste a smile on my face and get through the rest of the night just fine, holding it together until I can go upstairs with Keegan and see to his knuckles.

It's my turn to take care of him.

CHAPTER 12

"*Y*our knuckles look sore," I say the next morning as I help Keegan with the morning delivery. It's been a couple of days since the incident in the pub. Keegan didn't want me to clean up his knuckles for him. He just needed *me.*

And that didn't include sex. He wanted to hold me, to make sure I was safe and sound, all night.

And I was happy to be with him.

I don't know that I've felt so cherished and respected before.

But I wish he'd let me tend to the open cuts on his hand.

"They're not too bad."

I prop my hands on my hips. "I understand that you don't want me to make a big deal of it, but you don't get to lie to me about it either."

He glances up from his invoice and arches an

eyebrow. "Okay, they hurt like a bitch, is that what you're wanting to hear, Isabella?"

"Yes, actually, if it's the truth."

"There's no need to make a fuss." He sets the invoice on a box and glances around. "I don't know where I put the box cutter. I'll be right back."

He wanders out of the room, and I reach for the invoice. I quickly glance down the page and frown when he walks back into the room, box cutter in hand.

"What's wrong?" he asks.

"This must be a mistake. It says that you ordered five gallons of orange juice."

"No, that's right."

"I just dumped two gallons the other day because they'd gone bad, and we had like three more in the fridge."

"We order five gallons every week."

"But we don't *use* them. And it says you bought two cases of vodka, but there's still a lot of vodka out there under the bar. This is an Irish pub. People come here for Guinness and Irish whiskey."

"I know what kind of pub it is, love."

"I'm just saying that you didn't have to order this much stuff. We don't sell that many OJ drinks in a week."

"We have the standard order *every* week."

"There's at least a thousand-dollars-worth of liquor and other non-essentials that we won't use—or could have waited on for a week, Keegan."

"So now you know how to run a pub, then?" He folds his arms over his chest.

"No, not at all. But I minored in business in college, and I know my way around an invoice."

He rubs his hand over his mouth in agitation, and I don't understand why he's being so defensive about this. I'm just trying to help. To save him some money.

"I think you should stick to waiting tables and leave the bar ownership to me."

I purse my lips so I don't say something I'll regret later. I don't *have* to be here. I came to help him out, the way I've done for the past few weeks.

But I think it's best if I just go ahead and leave for a bit. I reach for my purse, set the invoice on a box, and turn to go.

But before I walk through the door, I turn back to him. "You know, it's kind of refreshing to know that you're not perfect, after all."

I let the door shut harder than needed behind me and march down the hall toward the front of the pub. Just as I pass the kitchen and glance inside, I see Fiona rubbing her shoulder.

"Are you okay, Fiona?"

"Oh, yes. This darn shoulder's been giving me fits. I must be lifting too much around here lately. I'll take something and be just fine."

I nod. "Okay, well, Keegan's in the storeroom if you need him. I'm going to head home for a bit."

"See you later, dear."

I may be pissed off at her son, but that's no reason to be unkind to Fiona. She might be the nicest person on Earth.

I'd parked my little car in front of the pub, so I hop in and hurry to Maggie's house. I still don't consider it home, even though Maggie's done nothing but make me feel welcome. Probably because I spend more time at Keegan's than I do here at Maggie's.

I cut the engine and stomp up the porch steps. When I get inside, I let my bag fall to the floor.

Maggie looks up from the book she's reading. "Hi there."

"Your brother is a jerk."

She sets the book aside and smiles. "Oh, for sure. Yeah. What did he do?"

"I mean, I was *not* trying to be bossy. I was only pointing some stuff out to him. Because I want to help, you know?"

"You're not making a lot of sense, but I'm with you, girl. Tell me more."

I pace the living room because I have too much energy to sit down. "We don't *need* five gallons of orange juice every week. It's not like we have a bunch of women coming in for brunch all the time for mimosas, for God's sake. We have people who want Guinness and whiskey, and sometimes a mixed cocktail."

"You're not wrong," Maggie says.

"He's so moody. He wouldn't let me help him with

his knuckles the other night, and today, he was kind of short with me—which is unlike him."

"Wait." She stands with me and holds up her hands. "You had a fight over *orange juice*?"

"Not just that. He also told me that I should stick to waiting tables and leave the pub ownership to him."

Her eyes go wide, and her lips form an O. "Did you slug him one?"

"No, I was quite calm. I left."

"Keegan's never liked being told what to do."

"I didn't *tell* him! I suggested that he buy less orange juice."

"So, you *did* fight over OJ."

I sigh. "I guess."

Maggie giggles.

"It isn't funny."

She giggles again, and I can't help but smile with her. "Okay, it's a little funny."

"Your first fight was over a breakfast drink. I think that's damn funny. Also, Keegan should be shot for telling you to stay in your lane."

"Yeah, that wasn't cool. But I was probably a little aggressive with my delivery, too. Maybe I should have said, '*I have a suggestion*,' before I criticized his vodka and OJ orders."

"So, are you going back over there to talk it out?"

I blow out a breath and flop onto the couch. "You know what? I don't think so. I'll go back when it's time for my shift."

"Good, we can ride together. Let's do a deep-cleansing face mask and pedicures."

"That's the best offer I've had in a long time."

A FEW HOURS LATER, at the start of my shift, I walk into the pub with freshly painted toes—albeit hidden in my sneakers—and a clean face. Keegan's behind the bar, stacking glasses. His head comes up and he looks right at me, his green eyes intense, and if I'm not mistaken, filled with regret.

Before either of us can say a word, Maggie approaches the bar with a grin. "Hey, Keegan, can I please have a glass of orange juice?"

I snort, unable to stop myself. Keegan's lips twitch.

"There's plenty back here, Mary Margaret, get it yourself. Izzy, I'd like to see you."

I follow him into the storeroom where this whole mess began, and he closes the door behind us.

"I owe you an apology," he begins. "I get defensive when it comes to my pub."

"Learned that the hard way," I mutter but smile up at him. "I should have been softer in my delivery. I wasn't trying to insult you or even tell you how to do your job."

"You were trying to help," he finishes for me and steps closer, dragging his hands up my arms and then frames my face. "And I was a jerk."

"Maybe we both had some jerk tendencies in that moment. But I don't think you're a jerk all the time."

His lips turn up in a smile before descending on mine. The kiss is possessive, sweet, and full of apology.

And when he pulls back, my knees are weak, and what I have on my mind is *not* going to work.

"We have to get back out there," I whisper.

"I know. Stay with me tonight."

"I planned on it."

He laughs and plants a kiss on my forehead. "I guess you weren't that mad at me, then."

"Oh, I was mad, but I knew we'd figure it out by this evening. I don't really hold much of a grudge. Unless you're my parents. Or Troy."

"It's good that I'm neither of those." He opens the door, and we find Fiona and Tom arguing in the hallway.

"It's a bloody stubborn arse that you are, Thomas O'Callaghan," Fiona says.

"Looks like arguments are going around today," Keegan observes. "What seems to be the problem?"

"I'm taking your mother into the doctor tomorrow for her shoulder, whether she likes it or not," Tom says, standing firm. I have a hunch he doesn't do this unless it's important.

Which tells me that Fiona's shoulder has been bothering her more than she's willing to admit.

"I just pulled something from lifting heavy bags of potatoes or some stupid thing," she insists.

"I'm with Da on this one," Keegan says. "You've been complaining about it for a while now. It's time to have it looked at."

"A bunch of bullies, the lot of you," Fiona mutters before storming off into the kitchen.

"It's a bully I am because I want to keep my wife healthy and strong." Tom shakes his head. "Women. I can't go a day without her, yet sometimes, I want to tumble her right into the sea."

I laugh as he walks away and lean my head on Keegan's biceps. "They're so lovely together."

"Even when they're mad, it's obvious they love each other. It was a good example to have growing up."

I nod and think about my parents and how I always knew they barely tolerated each other. What would it have been like to grow up with loving parents who doted on each other?

I shake my head. There's no sense dwelling on that since it is what it is.

"Hey, do you remember a couple of weeks ago when we were at the diner, and Cameron asked if he could speak to you and your brothers? Did you ever do that?"

Keegan's brow furrows. "No, now that you mention it, we didn't. I completely forgot about it. I'll ask Kane if he knows what's up."

"I don't know why that popped into my head this morning," I say. "And I was curious if you'd had the chance to talk."

"It's good having you around," he replies. "You're a great human *to-do* list."

"I have the memory of an elephant." I laugh and get to work.

"I CANNOT BELIEVE I burned my damn hand," Maeve says as she scowls at the gauze wrapped around her palm as the rest of us clean up from another busy evening. "What in the hell is wrong with me?"

"You've been working a lot of hours," I remind her.

"You need to take a few nights to yourself, Maeve," Keegan agrees. "I don't need to be taking up all of your spare time."

"What am I going to do, sit at home and binge Netflix?"

"That sounds lovely," I say. "But something tells me you're not the sit-and-watch-TV type."

"You'd be right." She cringes. "But I think I'll have to take you up on it because I can't grip drinks with this hand. Sorry, guys."

"Just take care of yourself," Keegan assures her.

We finish cleaning up the bar, and Keegan walks his sisters out to their cars. I go ahead and climb the stairs to the dwelling above. I like Keegan's apartment. It's very small, but it's comfortable. And it always makes me feel safe.

Maybe that's because it was literally my safe place after my world fell apart.

I've just peeled off my clothes and stepped into a warm shower when the bathroom door opens.

"I'm glad you feel at home here." He steps into the shower with me and immediately starts to wash my hair.

This is a little luxury I love. It always feels better when someone else washes your hair. And Keegan's hands are the best.

"I'm glad you don't mind that I make myself at home."

"If I minded, I wouldn't invite you up here. And we can't do this at Maggie's house. She'd barge right in."

I laugh and then sigh when his fingertips massage my scalp. "You're so good with your hands."

"Hmm."

He rinses my hair, and then kisses me long and slow while he ducks under the spray. I wash his back, his arms, his stomach.

"The first time I saw your abs, I thought that a woman could wash her clothes on them."

He lets out a laugh. "Is that so?"

"Yeah. Have you seen them?"

He glances down. "There they are."

"Bless them." I let my hands drift over each individual muscle. "I was never really an abs girl before. I mean, I could appreciate a flat stomach on a man, but it really wasn't a big deal. And then you took your shirt off, and I suddenly understood what all the fuss was about."

I glance up, expecting to see him scoff or laugh, but his face is suddenly serious.

"Did I say something wrong?"

"No." He kisses my forehead. The water runs down his torso, taking the soap away. He turns off the tap and reaches for a towel, wrapping me up in it. When I'm good and dry, he reaches for another, and I help him mop up the water.

He tosses the towels into a hamper, then takes me into his bedroom. A lamp is on low in the corner of the room, but the space is mostly bathed in shadows. The sun will start to rise in a few hours.

Keegan puts in a lot of hours in the pub. But he's never too tired to spend quality time with me after a long day of work.

He lays me down on the bed, and joins me, stretched out next to me. His fingers glide over my belly, which is definitely *not* as defined as his, and then up to my breasts.

"I've been with women before you," he says, at last, breaking the silence of the room. "I'm not innocent. But there was always something missing, something lacking. It made me believe that I wasn't cut out for a relationship. But then I met you, and I suddenly understood what all the fuss was about."

My eyes meet his in surprise. "That might be the nicest thing anyone's ever said to me."

He kisses my cheek, my chin, and then my lips as he links his fingers with mine and urges me onto my back.

"Everything about you is a new discovery. You make me crazy with wanting you. I can't keep my eyes off of you, Isabella. And it's going to sound macho, but I don't give a shit. You're mine. In every sense of the word, you're *mine*."

I moan and arch my back as he slides into me. This man—and everything he is—is pure decadence. He makes me feel feminine, desired, and *loved.*

And I should know because I've gone without love for a lot of my life.

My hands grip his ass as he moves faster, his strokes long and sure as he takes us both up and over the crest of pure sensation.

And when we're tangled together, the light extinguished, ready to fall asleep, Keegan kisses my hair, his arms wrapped around me from behind.

"I love you, Isabella."

I bite my lip and feel my eyes fill with tears. "I love you, too."

CHAPTER 13

"*M*ove in with me."

Izzy's eyes are wide over her coffee cup. I sprang the question on her just as she took a sip, and she starts to cough.

We get a few looks from others in the diner, but I don't care.

She covers her mouth with her napkin. Once she controls the coughing, she stares at me. "I'm sorry, I thought you just said to move in with you."

"That I did, lass."

She raises her mug back to her lips and takes a sip without coughing this time. "Are you sure that's what you want?"

I sit back in the booth, completely ignoring my oatmeal. "I wouldn't ask if it wasn't what I want. But if it's not what *you* want, you only have to say so."

She shakes her head, and I'm sure I'm about to get

shot down. But then she surprises me with, "I never stopped thinking of the apartment as home."

"If you weren't comfortable at Maggie's, you should have said so."

"I am comfortable there. I love Maggie. But it isn't home."

She takes a bite of her pancake, and I want to scoop her up and take her right here. But that would be frowned upon.

"Do you think it'll hurt Maggie's feelings if I move out?"

"I don't care, to be perfectly honest."

She laughs at me, and the sound makes all the hair stand up on my body. "Yes, you do."

"I don't think it'll hurt her feelings."

"Well, good. Because I don't want to do that. I'm grateful to her for letting me stay there. It's a really cute little house."

"Does this mean you're moving in with me, then?"

She blinks up at me. "Isn't that what we're talking about?"

"I asked, and then you started thinking and talking about Mary Margaret."

I now understand what my da meant when he said he'd like to toss Ma into the sea, and yet he can't live without her.

Izzy laughs and then wipes her mouth with her napkin. "Yes. I'm moving in."

"Today."

She continues laughing and then stares at me with a happy smile that lights up the entire diner. It's no wonder that I'm completely gone for her.

"I can go pack today and have a chat with Maggie."

"While you do that, I'll go over to the flat and clear out some space for your things."

"I've bought more things since I was there last."

"You can have the entire place if that's what you want."

"No, I think the purpose is to share the space. That's what moving in *together* means."

The waitress arrives with the check, and I give her my card before she can walk away.

Once I've paid, and we're in my truck, I take Izzy's hand and kiss her knuckles. "Thank you."

"For?"

"Moving in with me. Have you already forgotten?"

She's laughing again, and the sound makes my heart happy. "You don't have to thank me for that. Thank *you* for sharing your space."

"Our space."

She nods, and I pull in behind her little convertible at Maggie's.

"I'll be over in an hour or two. I'm not sure how long it'll take me to pack."

"Let me know if you need any help."

She leans over the center console for a quick kiss, and then she's out of the truck and walking up to the front door. Halfway there, she stops and blows me a kiss.

I'm going to marry her. Have wee babies with her, and build a home with her.

Maybe not in that order.

Now that she's in my life, I have no intention of ever letting her go.

The drive to the pub only takes five minutes. I hurry in through the back door, but before I climb the stairs to the flat, something tells me to go check on the kitchen.

It's just a feeling, a niggle at the back of my head, and I learned long ago to listen to feelings like that.

I push through the door of the kitchen and stop cold.

"Ma." I rush to my mother, who's doubled over and bracing herself on the counter. "What's wrong, Ma?"

"My chest," she groans. "And arm. My jaw. I don't know what to do."

I brace her in my arms as I pull my phone out of my pocket and immediately call 911.

"Emergency Services, what is your emergency?"

"I think my mother's having a heart attack. I need an ambulance straight away." I rattle off the address of the pub. "We're back in the kitchen. The front door is locked, but the back door is open."

"I'm dispatching now. Is she conscious?"

"Yes." I describe what she looks like—gray and sweaty, with shortness of breath. My heart is in my throat as I end the call with 911 and immediately dial Maeve's number.

"Hey," she says in greeting.

"Get Da and meet us at the hospital. My guess is we'll go to Seattle, but I don't know yet."

"What? What's happening?"

"Ma's having a heart attack." I guide her to a chair and help her down. "Ambulance is on the way. I can hear the sirens now."

"I hear them, too. Should we come to the pub?"

"I don't think you'll make it here in time."

I hear Maeve running through her house. "I can't find Da. Are you sure he's not at the pub?"

"I'm fucking sure, Maeve. I have to go."

I hang up as four EMTs hurry into the kitchen with a gurney and a whole host of equipment I know nothing about.

They nudge me out of the way as they immediately hook Ma up to machines that start to beep and flash.

"Definite heart attack," one of them says. "Let's load her up. We're flying her to Seattle General. We'll have her there in twenty minutes."

"I'm going with you."

Ma's eyes are closed, and she's wheezing as she struggles to breathe. We're loaded into the ambulance and rushed to a helipad where a helicopter is already running and ready for us. After we're transferred into the aircraft and strapped in, I put my headphones on to talk to the staff and then shoot off a group text to all of my siblings.

Me: *Ma and I are in a helicopter on our way to Seattle General. Heart attack. Please come right away.*

I hit send and reach out for her hand. I can't hear what she's saying because she's not wearing a headset, but I can read her lips.

Where's Tommy?

I lean down so I can talk into her ear.

"We're going to the hospital in Seattle, Mama. Da and the others are on their way. You're going to be okay."

Please, God, let her be okay.

I've never been so scared in my life as the helicopter touches down on the roof of the hospital, and we're rushed inside and down to the emergency department.

"Fiona O'Callaghan," someone yells. "Female, sixty-two. Chest pain, left arm pain, and jaw pain."

"Got it," someone else yells as Ma is wheeled back to a room. I stand back and watch as a flurry of people surround her and immediately hook her up to an IV and all kinds of monitors.

"Pulse is one eighty-one."

"We need to get that down."

I approach her from the side, hoping to help calm her. "Ma. I'm right here. I'm not going anywhere."

I take her hand once more, and she looks over at me with wide eyes. "I want Tommy."

"I know, and he's coming." *I want him, too.* "For now,

these people are going to help you. And I'm right beside you. I won't budge. You know how stubborn I am."

She licks her lips with nervousness.

They whisk her away for an x-ray, making me out to be a liar because I can't be with her, but then she's brought back.

Her coloring is worse. She looks scared out of her mind.

Jesus, I don't know what to do for her. I've never felt so helpless in all my life.

After what feels like hours, I hear my father behind me.

"I'm here," he says and hurries over to us. *Thank Christ.* "I'm here, darlin'. Oh, my love, I'm so sorry. There now, it's going to be just fine."

"Tommy." Ma clings to my father and finally lets the tears fall. "I'm so scared."

"Shh. There now." He kisses her forehead and looks up at the doctor. "What's happening?"

"She's having a massive heart attack," he says. "We're about to wheel her in for an angiogram so we can see where the heart is failing. If need be, we'll perform surgery. I need permission to do so."

"I'm her husband, and you have permission." He kisses Ma's cheek. "He's going to fix you up right as rain, me love."

When they wheel her off for surgery, Da and I walk out to the waiting room where everyone sits, waiting.

Izzy, with eyes full of tears, immediately jumps up and wraps her arms around my stomach, her cheek pressed to my chest, and I've never felt so relieved in all my life to see another human being.

The lump that was in my throat eases a bit.

"I'm so sorry," she whispers. "I hate that you had to go through that by yourself."

"She's going to be okay." I kiss the top of her head and look over at the others. "She's going in for an angiogram so they can see what's going on. She's definitely having a heart attack."

"Oh, Da." Maggie hugs our father, and Maeve joins them, rubbing his back supportively.

"She's going to be better than ever," Da says as he pastes a cheerful smile on his weathered face. I've never seen him more worried or look so old. But he's trying to be optimistic for us.

"Jace is the surgeon," Anastasia says. She holds the baby against her shoulder. "He's going to keep her completely safe. I'd trust no one more than Jace. He saved my father's life just a couple of years ago."

"See?" Maggie says. "She's going to be just fine."

Jace is Anastasia's brother-in-law. We've met him several times at family gatherings. I've never taken the time to sit down to talk with him, but if Stasia trusts him, so do I.

"We should sit." I urge Da toward a chair. We're gathered as a family in the corner of a big waiting room.

"Actually," a nurse says as she approaches, "if you'd like a more private place for your family to wait, there's a waiting room over here that might be better."

She leads us just around a corner and opens a door. The light comes on to reveal a private waiting area, just the right size for our group.

"Don't worry, I'll let the staff know you're in here so you won't miss any news."

"Thank you," I say to her.

I sit, and Izzy sits next to me. Shawn and Lexi are across from us with Kane and Anastasia. Maeve, Maggie, and Da take up the rest of the seats.

"Did they say how long it would take?" Maeve asks.

"No."

"This is the worst part," Shawn says and rubs his face with agitation. "The waiting."

"I'll go get coffees," Maggie says. "Does everyone want coffee from the cafeteria?"

"They have an espresso cart not too far from here," Stasia says. "I drank a lot of coffee from it. I would come help, but—"

"No, you sit," Maggie says. She takes orders for three other coffees and then sets off in search of caffeine.

"Maggie needs to have a task," Da says. "She's a doer. If there's ever a crisis, she's the one bustling about."

"I knew something wasn't right," Maeve says softly. "I had a hunch that it wasn't just a tweaked shoulder, but she kept insisting that she was fine. That stubborn woman."

"None of us knew," I remind her. "It's not your fault."

"It's my fault," Da says. "For not making her go to the damn doctor."

"It's nobody's fault," Izzy repeats and rubs Da's arm. She holds my hand tightly with her other hand.

Anastasia shifts the baby and then frowns at her husband. "Would you please take him for a minute? He's only eight pounds, but he starts to get heavy."

"Of course, love."

"May I hold him?" Izzy asks. "I've meant to come see you, but something always comes up."

"You're more than welcome to hold him," Kane says as he brings the baby to Izzy and gently lays him in her arms. "He's been a little fussy today, so if you need his binky, we have it ready."

"Aww, are you fussy, little love?" She kisses Thomas's head and smiles down at him. "He's already changed so much in such a short period of time."

"I swear, he changes every day," Stasia agrees. "Yesterday, I thought he looked more like me. This morning, he smiled just like Kane. And about an hour ago, he looked like an alien."

"He's too little to smile," Kane insists. "It was probably gas."

We laugh a little, the mood lightening a bit with talk of the baby.

"No, you don't look like an alien," Izzy says. The baby is awake now and watching Izzy talk to him. "You're an amazing little man. Yes, you are."

He opens his mouth as if searching for a snack. "I think he's hungry."

"I don't think I can help you with that." Izzy kisses his forehead again.

"Here." Kane pulls a bottle out of the baby bag and shakes up some formula. "You can help."

He passes her the bottle, along with a spit rag.

"I do breastfeed, as well, but I wasn't producing enough, so we had to supplement with formula."

"Nothing wrong with that," Izzy says, watching the baby as she feeds him.

My stomach felt tight when I saw her holding him at the hospital before, and it's even more so now. But before I can say anything, Maggie returns with the coffee orders.

Not long after, there's a knock at the door, and Jace walks into the waiting area. He's in scrubs, a stethoscope around his neck.

"Hi, everyone. I think we've all met, but if not, I'm Jace. Anastasia's brother-in-law. When she was first presented, we thought Mrs. O'Callaghan was having a major heart attack due to the severity of her symptoms. But once we got in there with an angiogram, we discovered that this was actually a *minor* cardiac event."

He goes on to show us images of Ma's heart and indicates where an artery was clogged.

"She's been having symptoms for a long time," Maeve admits. "And she blew it off, saying it was a sore shoulder."

"That's pretty common, especially in women. She's likely been suffering with this for a little while given how blocked that artery was. But we were able to put a little balloon in there to open it up, and I placed a stent in the artery so it can't get blocked again."

"So, no major surgery?" I ask.

"No, I don't see the need for that. She'll be on blood thinners for a while and other medications. She'll want to eat a more heart-healthy diet. I already told her, no more meat pies for a bit. I'm going to keep her here for a couple of days for observation, and then she'll be ready to go home. I'll send a whole list of instructions home with her."

"Thank you." Da stands and shakes Jace's hand, then pulls him in for a hug. "You just saved her life, and she's the most important person in the world."

"You're very welcome. That's what we're here for. Now, do I get to peek at the baby?"

Anastasia laughs, and Izzy stands so Jace can get a better view of the little guy.

"Joy's going to be jealous."

"Joy's seen him," Stasia says with a laugh. "She told me not to tell you because you'd be jealous."

"Joy and I are going to have a little conversation later." He sounds serious, but he's laughing when he places the baby back in Izzy's arms and then kisses Stasia on the cheek. "Good job, Mama."

"Thanks."

"If you have any questions about Fiona, I'm here all day, and the nursing staff is incredible."

"When can I see her?" Da asks.

"She's being moved into her room now. Once they have her settled, you can all see her. But because there are so many of you, let's rotate you through, okay? Tom, you're welcome to stay with her, but the others will have to take turns."

"That's the story of our lives," Kane says. "We've mastered taking turns. Thank you again."

"You're welcome. Now, go spoil her rotten."

"Oh," I say as Da stands to go see her, "we will."

CHAPTER 14

This is my first day off in a long while. Keegan gave me strict instructions this morning to stay away from the pub all day, and I'm not exactly sure what to do with myself. Even on the days I don't have a shift waiting tables, I still go in to help out in some way.

I've turned into somewhat of a workaholic.

Mostly, I enjoy the atmosphere in the pub—the sounds and laughter. And I like being close to Keegan and his siblings.

I finally feel accepted by a family.

But today, I've been kicked out. So, I decided to get on the ferry and go to Seattle to see Fiona.

She's been in the hospital for three days, and I want to go and check on her. After checking in at the visitors' desk, I make my way up to Fiona's room.

I knock on the door and am surprised to find Fiona alone when I push inside.

"Hey there," I say with a smile. "Where's Tom?"

She grins over at me like a young girl. Her cheeks are rosy, and her green eyes are bright. "He went to get me some things so I can go home today."

"They're releasing you?" I sit next to her and set my handbag on the floor next to me.

"They are, and I'm going to surprise the kids. They don't know. I'm just going to walk into the pub like I own the place."

I chuckle with her. "This is exciting. Congratulations. I'm so relieved that you're healthy, Fiona. We've all been worried sick."

"I hate that I caused so much worry. It's a mother's job to soothe her children, not scare them."

"They love you," I remind her. "They all love you very much. And I have to admit, I've grown rather attached to you myself."

"What a lovely thing to say." She reaches over and pats my hand. "And it's attached that I've grown to you, as well, Izzy. You're a sweet woman."

She shifts in the bed, and I can see that she wants to say more. "What is it?"

"Well, I'm a protective mother, you see. And I guess I'm wondering what you see happening between you and Keegan in the long term."

"You're asking me my intentions with your son?"

She laughs a little and then shrugs a shoulder. "Indeed, I am."

I look down at my hands and then up at her again, letting the words start to tumble out of me. "I'm completely in love with him. When I first met him, I thought he was grouchy, but he's not. He's just a thinker. And he's funny. Incredibly kind. He loves his family so much. And he's thoughtful. He's *good* to me, you know?"

"He'd better be, or he'd have to answer to me," she says. "And it's clear to me that he loves you just as much, my dear. I don't think I've ever seen Keegan this devoted to a woman. But you're young. Much younger than him."

"I guess there's a bit of an age gap." I sit back, thinking about it. "About seven years, I suppose. But we're both adults."

"Yes, but are you sure this is what you're going to want for the long term? Keegan's life is on that island. In the pub. He loves it, almost as much as he loves you."

"I love the pub, too. I was just thinking that when I walked up here. He made me take the day off, and I'm a little lost."

"I'm glad you enjoy your job, but is it what you want forever?"

I frown at Fiona, wondering what I'm missing here.

"Perhaps I'm not asking this right. I guess what I'm saying is, I know you've likely had other dreams for yourself. To have a career, for example."

"I can still do that. I've applied for a few jobs here in the Northwest. And, yes, I'll have to commute a bit, but it's a compromise, right? All relationships have them. And if I don't get one of those jobs, then it just wasn't meant to be. I *love* your family, and I've never felt so content or welcomed in my life. I'm not willing to give that up for anything."

"You *are* welcome with us, Izzy." Fiona smiles softly. "And I think you're right. You can certainly have both. I'm glad we got to have this conversation."

Before I can reply, my phone starts to ring. When I check it, I don't recognize the number.

"I'm sorry, Fiona, I should answer this. Hello?"

"May I speak with Izzy Harris?"

"This is Izzy."

"Hello, this is Roger Johnston at KXLY TV in Seattle. We reviewed your resume and your audition video, and if you're still looking for a job, we'd like to hire you."

I stare at Fiona, blinking slowly. "Without an interview?"

Roger chuckles on the other end. "I'm going to be honest here. Someone quit unexpectedly, and we need to fill the position immediately. We'd need you on-air on Saturday."

"That's in three days."

"Yes, it is. So, we ran a background check and called the references you provided, and we're comfortable moving forward quickly. If you're available."

I swallow hard. Fiona's smiling like crazy at me now.

"Izzy?"

"I'm sorry, this is such a crazy surprise. Yes, I'm available."

"Great. Come into the studio on Friday so I can show you around. I'll have you sign some paperwork and such. And then we'll start bright and early on Saturday. This will be a part-time position, with you reporting the weather on-air in the studio on Saturday and Sunday. We will send you out on remote sometimes, as well. You'll also be filling in during the week whenever our senior meteorologist is on vacation."

"This is unexpected and incredible. Thank you for the opportunity, Roger."

"You're welcome. I'm going to send you an email with everything you'll need to know. I'll talk to you soon, Izzy."

"Okay, thanks again. Goodbye."

I hang up and stare at Fiona, and then I do the happiest happy dance anyone has ever seen. Fiona claps and lets out a loud *WHOOP*!

"I got a job!"

"Yes, you did. I'm so proud of you, Izzy."

"Oh my gosh, I have so much to do. I have to get some clothes—I don't have a wardrobe appropriate for TV. And I have to tell Keegan. I'm going to surprise him."

"So many surprises today," she says. "I love it.

Surprises keep us young. I won't say a word to anyone. You go do some shopping and enjoy your day off, and then you can tell everyone else."

"Thank you." I rush over and kiss her cheek. "Thank you for sharing this with me."

"It's an honor and a privilege, and that's the truth of it."

"I can stay until Tom gets back."

"Tom is here," he says as he walks in carrying a small bag full of Fiona's things.

"I can't stay." I kiss his cheek and then wrap him up in a hug. "I love you, Tom. I love you both. And I'll see you later."

"Well." Tom blushes like crazy, and Fiona laughs. "Okay, then."

"Bye!"

"Have fun," Fiona calls after me as I hurry out of the room.

Where do I go? I don't know Seattle all that well. I could call Maggie or Maeve, but they're both helping Keegan at the pub today.

And then I remember that Samantha Nash gave me her number at Anastasia's baby shower and extended an open invitation to reach out to her anytime.

It's still crazy to me that I have Leo Nash's wife's phone number.

When I get to my car, I pull up the number and shoot her a text.

Me: *Hey! This is Izzy Harris, we met at Anastasia's baby* *shower. I don't know if you were serious about meeting up sometime but I'm currently in Seattle, and if you're free, I'd like to see you! Ignore if this is weird. LOL*

I take a deep breath and let it out slowly.

I have a brand-new weather job, doing what I've always dreamed of. And I got it on my own merit, without my father making any phone calls.

And I start in a few days.

I'm so *nervous*.

My phone starts to ring in my hand.

"Hey, it's Sam," she says when I answer. "This is perfect timing. I'm at the downtown studio with Leo today because he's helping a band with some recording, and I could honestly use a break. We're across the street from Succulent Sweets. How do you feel about cupcakes?"

"I've never turned down a cupcake in my life."

"You're my kind of girl. Where are you now?"

"Seattle General hospital."

"Okay, you're about fifteen minutes away. Just plug the bakery into your GPS and you'll find it no problem."

"Awesome, I'll see you soon. Thanks, Sam."

I end the call and do exactly as she suggested. And she's not wrong. The bakery is easy to find and in a super cute part of downtown, surrounded by a mix of restaurants, shops, and offices. I remember Matt's wife, Nic, telling me at the shower that she owns this place. I can't wait to try her cupcakes.

I find a spot to park and walk into Succulent Sweets. It's designed similar to an old-fashioned café, with white-tiled floors and little round tables set about. A wide array of gorgeous cupcakes fill the glass counter.

I see Nic and Sam chatting by the cash register.

"Hello, ladies." I grin as I approach them. They greet me with immediate warmth.

They weren't lying when they said the Montgomerys are a welcoming family.

"I'm *so* glad you texted me," Sam says. "I love Leo's music, and I enjoy studio time, but it's been a long day over there."

"Cupcakes usually fix that," Nic says. "You look wonderful, Izzy."

"Thank you, I feel wonderful. I got a job today." I tell them all about my new job here in Seattle as a meteorologist, and when I'm finished, they each offer me high-fives.

"That's *so* cool," Sam says.

"I need to shop," I admit. "I need a whole new wardrobe for this. And I don't know where to go."

Sam and Nic share a look, and then Sam reaches for her phone. "Don't worry. We've got this covered." She taps on the screen and then puts the phone on speaker as it rings.

"Hello?"

"Hey, Nat, I'm here with Nic and Izzy. You remember Izzy from Stasia's party?"

"Of course! Hi, guys."

"Hi," Nic and I say in unison.

"Listen," Sam continues, "we have a wardrobe emergency."

"Does this require shopping?" Nat asks.

"Of course, it does."

"I'm your girl," Nat replies. "I can have a sitter here in thirty minutes."

"We're going to need Jules, too," Sam adds. "We'll meet you at her office."

"Whoa, this is some emergency," Nat says.

"It's a Defcon One," Sam agrees. "See you soon."

"I can't go." Nic sighs sadly. "I have to sell cupcakes."

"Your job is important," Sam assures her. "And I need three of the chocolate. I'll take a dozen assorted over to the studio, as well."

"And for you?" Nic asks. "You *have* to celebrate with a cupcake."

"I want a chocolate, a strawberry, and I want to try the funfetti."

"I really like her," Sam says to Nic with a grin as Nic fills our order. When we're loaded down with our sweets, we leave the bakery and walk across the street to the studio.

"Hey," Sam greets Leo as we walk in. "You're not recording?"

"I needed a break. They're driving me nuts. But you brought me cupcakes."

"You have to share with everyone," Sam warns him.

"Like hell." Leo opens the box and bites into a lemon, then smiles at me. "Hey there, Iz."

No one has called me Iz since I arrived, and I have to admit, I don't hate it coming from Leo's sexy mouth.

"Hi, Leo."

"I have to go help Izzy shop for a wardrobe for her new job. We're going with Nat and Jules."

"What's the new job?" he asks me.

"I'll be reporting the weather for a local news station."

His eyes light up. "No shit? That's fucking awesome. I'm practically related to a weather girl. Good job, Iz."

"Thanks." I feel my cheeks flush. Leo Nash is praising me and looking at me like he's proud of me, and I feel sixteen all over again.

But Keegan's ten-times hotter. Leo's sexy as all get out, but my man is incredible. And I can't wait to see him.

"Okay, we have to run. See you at home later." Sam forgets to kiss Leo, and he catches her wrist and tugs her into his arms. The kiss he plants on her is hot with a capital H.

"Have fun, sunshine."

She smiles, brushes a piece of hair off her cheek, and we head out.

"He still gives me butterflies," she mutters when we're out the door. "Don't tell him I said that."

"I totally get it. And not because of Leo, but because of Keegan."

She turns surprised blue eyes over to me. "Well, that's awesome."

"Yeah, it's better than awesome."

"Good for you. A new man and a new job."

"A new life."

"Attagirl."

"HOLY SHIT, YOU GUYS CAN *SHOP*."

We've finished with our shopping spree and are grabbing a glass of wine and a light dinner before we go our separate ways.

"It's our best skill," Jules agrees. "But you have to look your best on Saturday."

"Absolutely," Nat chimes in.

"I still can't believe everything I was able to get on my budget."

"The Rack and Saks Off Fifth are lifesavers," Sam says. "You can get so much there for a fraction of the cost. And you look *amazing* in everything you got. I totally covet your tits."

"You have really good boobs," Natalie agrees.

"I had to buy mine," Jules says. "So, I'm jealous, too."

I laugh and take a bite of a crab cake. "You guys are good for my ego."

"Okay, you've told us all about the new job. Tell us more about the man. We've all met Keegan several times, and he's super nice, but also a bit quiet." Jules sips her wine. "Spill it."

"Use all the dirty words," Nat agrees.

I can't stop laughing at these girls. "You guys are fun. Well, he's hot."

"Does he have a big penis?" Sam asks.

"Yes."

"Right on." Jules gives me a fist bump.

"He's also really *nice.*" I tell them how he just took me in after I left Troy, and how I didn't have a choice but to fall in love with him.

He's *everything.*

"You have balls, girl. It takes some guts to know what you do and don't want and walk out of a wedding like that."

"I felt like a coward," I admit.

"No way," Nat says. "You did what you needed to do to be safe and to stand up for yourself. There is nothing cowardly about that. And I hope my daughters would do the same thing."

"And now you have this incredible life that you've made for yourself," Jules adds. "A great guy, a family who's accepted you and loves you, and this killer new job."

"And some awesome new friends," I remind them all. "Thank you for helping me today. I had a blast."

"If you ever want to shop or eat or talk about boys, we're your girls." Natalie glances at her phone. "And Luke says hi."

"Nate texted, too. Stella's staying with my parents tonight, and he's taking me out on a date."

"You all landed some hot men yourselves."

"Hell yes, we did, honey," Sam says. "And it's damn awesome."

THE ONLY BAD thing about living on an island is that it takes so long to get home when you're anxious to get there.

I swear, the ferry was extra slow this evening.

I'm excited to tell everyone the good news, but I want to tell Keegan first.

When I walk through the back door, I can hear that things are in full swing in the pub. So, I haul all of my bags upstairs and dump them onto the bed. They're damn heavy.

And I have no idea where I'm going to hang everything. We're bursting at the seams as it is.

But we'll figure it out.

I hurry downstairs and slide behind the bar. I walk up behind Keegan and slip my arms around his waist to hug him.

"You best get out of here. My girlfriend will be back any minute."

"Haha, very funny."

He turns and offers me a quick kiss. "You look like you had fun today."

"I had *so* much fun, and I have a million things to tell you."

"My ma's home."

"I know." I grin at him. "I went up to see her, and she was waiting to be released."

"And you didn't tell me?"

"She wanted it to be a surprise. Hey, if it dies down at all, or you're able to sneak away for a second, will you come upstairs for just a few? I have some fun news, and I want to tell you first."

"Sure thing, love."

"Awesome." I kiss his arm and then make my way back upstairs. I'm standing in the middle of the bedroom, staring at the pile of bags on the bed, when Keegan walks in.

"Did some shopping today, did you?"

I laugh and look at him helplessly. "I didn't realize I bought so much. But there's a reason. I know you have to get back, but I wanted to tell you right away."

"Are you okay, love?"

"I'm *great.* Remember when I told you that I applied for some meteorologist positions?"

"Yes."

"I got one. I got a job. In Seattle. I know it's going to be a bit of a commute, but it's only part-time, so it'll be doable. I needed clothes for television, so I called Samantha Nash, and we ended up spending the day with Natalie and Jules, and they know all the best places to get the good stuff for a fraction of the cost, and oh my God, Keegan, I got a *job*!"

He's grinning from ear to ear, his arms crossed over his chest as he listens to me babble. And finally, when I stop talking, he pulls me to him and spins me around in celebration.

"I'm so fucking proud of you, Isabella."

"Even though I'll have to cut back on my hours just a little bit here? I'll be at the station on Saturdays and Sundays, super early in the morning, so—"

"Baby, this is what you want. This is your dream. I can always find more help here. The important thing is that you got exactly what you wanted."

I wrap my arms around his neck and bury my face against his shirt, breathing him in. "I couldn't have done it without you."

"Yes, you could have." He kisses my cheek. "But it's happy I am that I'm here to support you through it. Way to go, love."

I kiss his neck and bite his earlobe, suddenly wanting him more than I ever have.

It's as if he just *knows* because he props me up against the wall, my legs wrapped around his waist, and kisses me senseless.

I push against him, rubbing my core against his hardness through two layers of denim.

Suddenly, he sets me on my feet and pushes my jeans down my hips, then turns me around and urges me to bend over.

"Grab the wall."

I do as he says, and he pushes right inside me, taking me on a fast and hard ride. It's over as quickly as it began, but I'm sated and humming with satisfied energy.

"Well, that's the perfect thing to add to this day," I say as I pull my jeans back up. "Want me to come down and help?"

"No." He kisses me softly this time. "I want you to unpack your beautiful new things and find homes for them. Order something from the kitchen if you like. And relax."

"You spoil me."

"That's the goal."

CHAPTER 15

"**G**ood morning," Izzy says as she rolls over and smiles up at me with blue eyes heavy with sleep. "You're dressed."

"I am. I have to run over to Kane's. I'm going to have that chat with Cameron we talked about a while ago. I didn't want to wake you."

"It's okay. Good luck with your talk."

"Do you want me to make you some coffee before I go?"

She cups my cheek gently. "You're the sweetest. That's not necessary but thank you."

"Okay, I'll see you later." I kiss her, then have to pull away before I say *fuck Cameron* and get back into bed with her.

The drive to Kane's property isn't far. Cameron's and Shawn's cars are already in the driveway when I pull in.

I walk around the house to the back and enter through the sunporch. Just as I expected, the men are gathered in the kitchen, drinking coffee.

"I'm going to need some of that." I walk right to the coffee maker and brew myself a cup of joe, and when I've added some milk, I turn to them. "Good morning."

"It's damn early," Shawn says.

"I know, and I appreciate you both getting up early. I know you work late at night." Cameron takes a drink from his mug. "I've been meaning to talk with you three for a while, and it seems something always comes up. First, how's Ma?"

"She's going to be fine," Kane says. "Scared the hell out of us, but she's fine."

"Good."

Our mother practically raised Cameron through his teenage years. His dad was barely around, and his mom left when he was small. We're his family.

"What's up, Cam?" Shawn inquires.

"Are you going to ask if you can marry Maggie?" Kane asks.

"Not today," Cam replies and drags his hand down his face. The three of us narrow our eyes. "I want to run something by you. I'm ending my government contract, effective in thirty days. Which means, for the first time since I was eighteen, I won't be tied to Uncle Sam."

"What made you decide to do this?" I ask him.

"I want to come home. Maggie's right. I'm in and

out way too much. I'm on the downslope to forty. I want to set down roots and be here more. Shit, Ma had a heart attack, and I was in Tel Aviv. It's a little hard to get home from the Middle East in an emergency. It fucking sucked."

"You were in Israel?" Shawn asks. "What the hell?"

"You know I can't tell you why," Cam says quietly. "And that's the other thing that's getting old. I can't even confide in you guys about the stuff that goes on. Everything about my life is a fucking secret. In the beginning, that was part of the fun of it. Now, it's just…old."

"What are you going to do?" I ask.

"I'm going to work as a contractor with some major corporations—and, yes, some big government agencies —on their IT security. So, while the government will still be paying me, they're not my boss anymore. Also, there's a lot more money in the private sector."

Cam is a genius when it comes to computers. That's all any of us knows about his job.

"Are you asking for help with the startup costs?" Kane asks.

"No, I have the money. I'm just asking for your thoughts on this. Is it the smart thing to do? Am I stupid to walk away from the seniority and stability I have with my current job, even if I'm growing to hate it with each passing day?"

"We don't know anything about your job," Shawn reminds him. "But if it's making you miserable, and this is where you want to live full-time, it's not the wrong thing to do."

"I agree."

"Are you doing this for Mary Margaret?" Kane asks as he watches his best friend thoughtfully.

"Partially," Cam admits. "But even if she told me to fuck right off, which she does on the regular, I'd still want this. I'm too old to spend every night in a different country, worried it might be the day I'm assassinated."

"Fucking Christ," I mutter.

"Then do it," Kane says. "Coming home is never the wrong answer. If you hate it, you can always go back."

"No," Cam says, shaking his head. "That's not how it works."

"Come home," Shawn says.

"This is where you belong, mate" I agree. "Always has been, always will be. We have your back."

He nods and then grins. "I'm going to need a place to live."

"We have Maeve for that," Kane says. "If you need a place to crash in the meantime, you can stay here."

"With the screaming baby?" Cam asks, just as we hear the baby crying upstairs. "I'm sure I can find a place."

"There's always the cabin," Shawn says. "I know it's far away, but it's there if you want it."

"I'll grab a rental here on the island," Cam replies. "It won't be a problem. I'm not going to stay with my dad, that's for sure. And the hotel I usually use is fucking expensive. Anyway, thank you. I needed to talk it out. To make sure I wasn't out of my mind."

"I don't think you are. Well, not over this." I pat him on the shoulder.

"I have to catch a flight to D.C.," Cam says and stands up.

"I have some writing to do while the story is fresh in my head," Shawn adds.

"I'm going to stay behind and talk with Kane."

We say our goodbyes to the other two, and then Kane and I take our coffee out to the sunporch.

"Izzy starts her new job tomorrow," I say as we stare out at the ocean beyond.

"And we're ready," Kane replies. "It's going to be a hell of a party."

"Izzy has no idea. It's perfect. Thanks for hosting."

"It's our pleasure. Stasia isn't feeling up to going out too much yet, so it works out well for us. What's on your mind, Keegan?"

I set my coffee aside and run my hand through my hair. "Have you given any more thought to selling the property we looked at?"

"I have. Have you decided that you want it, then?"

"I do." I turn to my brother now, the person I trust most in the world. "I want to build a house on it. I'm going to ask her to marry me."

His lips tip up in a smile. "I'm happy for you, brother."

"I never expected this turn of events, and that's the truth. But I can't see myself without her. And she deserves better than the tiny flat above the pub."

"Has she complained?"

"Not once. But Christ, Kane, I don't know how our parents raised us all up there for as long as they did. It's tight with just Izzy and me. And I want to give her a pretty house that she can fuss over."

"Of course, you do. Da wanted that for Ma, as well. That's why he bought her the house as soon as he could. If you can afford to give her more, why would you stay at the pub?"

"Well, that's the sticky part. Let's talk price."

"I'm not going to sell the land to you, Keegan. For a couple of reasons. First, you couldn't afford it. Ocean-front property on this island goes for a million an acre, easy. And secondly, you're my brother. I love you."

"You won't sell me the land because you love me?"

"That's right. I'll gift two acres to you."

"No." I stand, but Kane stands with me and lays his hand on my shoulder.

"Hear me out. I'll gift it to you, and I'll never buy you another birthday or Christmas gift again, if that's the way you want it. I won't pay for the house to be built, that's on you."

"I don't want you to pay for any of it, Kane. I said before, you don't pay my way. I don't give a rat's ass that you have more money than God himself."

"What am I going to do with all of it if I can't bless

me family with it, as well?" he counters, his Irish up. "It means nothing if I can't share it with the people I love. If it's two measly acres you want, out of the twenty I own—which is more than I need—you can bloody well *have* them! Because you'll be nearby with your family, and it'll bring joy to you and to me at the same time."

I sit back down and stare out at the ocean. How am I supposed to argue with that?

"I'd like to bring her out here to make sure she likes the property before we make it legal and I hire someone to draw up the plans."

"Of course," Kane says.

"Are you going to be a pain in the arse neighbor?"

My brother laughs and drinks the last of his coffee. "Hell yes, I am."

"The Emerald City is going to enjoy these nice warm temperatures for the next few days, but then this low-pressure system that's currently sitting up here off the coast of Alaska will head our way, bringing us some cool air and dropping us down into the forties for the weekend. Sorry, folks, I'm just the messenger. Now, I want you to stay safe around the water as we're calling for high waves with that wind…"

"She's so damn good," Maeve says. We're all gathered at Kane's house to watch Izzy's debut on television.

What we're watching now is the repeat. This particular station runs the morning news twice. Live from five to seven in the morning, and then again from seven to nine.

It was too damn early to ask everyone to meet at five.

But no one balked at coming to watch the seven-o'clock show.

Of course, I was pinned to the TV at the flat at five, and I didn't miss a minute of Izzy's weather report.

"That red dress is smoking hot on her," Maggie says.

I couldn't agree more.

The dress fits her like a glove. Her makeup is heavier than I'm used to seeing on her, and her long, blond hair is down around her shoulders and teased into long waves.

"Izzy, isn't there something you can do about that weekend forecast?" the weekend anchor, Chuck, asks her.

Izzy chuckles and shrugs her shoulders in apology. "I'm sorry, Chuck, but the good news is, once this bout of cooler weather subsides, we'll be back in the sixties with some nice sunshine for several days."

"That is good news. Thank you, Izzy, and welcome again. We're happy to have you."

"Thank *you*, Chuck."

The anchor bids everyone farewell for the day, and I get a text on my phone.

Izzy: *Just getting off the ferry. Should be home soon.*

I grin and reply.

Me: *Just come over to Kane's. I came to see the baby.*

It's not a complete lie. The baby is here. Currently being held by my mother.

"Izzy's just getting off the ferry. I told her to come here."

"My breakfast charcuterie spread is ready," Maeve says as she hurries to the dining room table nearby. "I just have to grab the fruit from the fridge."

"What in the hell is a charcuter board?" I ask.

"Charcuter*ie*," she corrects me. "It's usually a fancy cheese and crackers tray, but I made it for breakfast, so it has waffles and fruit and all the toppings, along with bacon and eggs and a complete mimosa bar."

"I'm hungry," Shawn says, making his way to the table, but Maeve slaps his hand. "Ouch."

"You can't eat until Izzy gets here."

Maeve, Maggie, Lexi, and Anastasia fuss with the balloons that spell *CONGRATS* on the wall, and we're all armed with noisemakers when the woman of the hour walks through the door.

"Congratulations!" we all yell and make our noise, and I watch in horror as the woman I love disolves into tears.

"Whoa. No, no, no. Don't cry, love." I open my arms, and she walks right into them and buries her face in my chest. "Shh, don't cry. I'm sorry you didn't want a party, I didn't know."

"I want a party," she mutters against my shirt. "It's just I'm so grateful and so *tired.*"

She steps back and wipes away her tears.

"You did so great," Kane says and pulls her in for his own hug. "You're a superstar, darling."

"Pass her around," Da says, taking my girl from Kane. "It's a lovely woman you are, Izzy me darlin'. I'm so proud of you."

"You're all making me cry." Izzy sniffs. "Oh my gosh, this is so amazing."

Everyone takes their turn, hugging her and fussing over her. Finally, Lexi asks her, "What time did you have to get up this morning?"

"One," Izzy replies. "I had to be at the studio by three, and we were on the air at five."

"Damn," Shawn says. "You were up before the pub even closed."

"Yeah." She wipes her tears dry and takes in all the balloons and food. "Oh, you guys. This is amazing. Thank you so much."

"We watched every minute of it," Ma says. "We all sat together, right here, and watched you. You were wonderful, Izzy. Smart and sassy, and as beautiful as the sun."

"I just stopped crying," Izzy says and tears up again. "I was so nervous. But it was exhilarating. And so *fun.* Everyone there is really nice, and I even have my own little cubicle, which I didn't expect since I'm only part-time. And I have to admit, I'm glad it's part-time.

Because while it's *amazing*, I also love the pub, and this way, I can do both."

"It's not often a person can do everything they love," Da says and pats Izzy's shoulder. "Good for you."

"A celebration drink," Maggie says and passes Izzy a champagne glass full of orange juice and bubbly.

I can't help but chuckle every time I see orange juice now.

"To Izzy, the best weather girl Seattle's ever seen," I say with my glass raised.

"To Izzy!" everyone says and takes a drink from their glasses.

Izzy scrunches up her nose. "I think my tummy is still nervous. I'd better just have OJ. God knows I don't need any more coffee."

We settle in with food and drinks, chatting about Izzy's first day. After everything is cleaned up, and we've taken lots of pictures for social media, and everyone has snuggled the baby, people start to leave, to go about their days.

When Izzy and I are left with Kane and Anastasia, I turn to the love of my life and eye her heels. "Do you have more sensible shoes in your car?"

"Just flip-flops. That's all I grabbed this morning."

"I have sneakers you can borrow," Stasia offers, "if they'll fit."

Thankfully, they do, and I lead Izzy outside and along the cliffs.

"It's beautiful out here," she says. "You just can't beat the view."

"No, you can't." When we reach the place where Kane and I talked before, I stop her. "What do you think of this?"

She turns to the water, but I shake my head, brace her shoulders in my hands, and turn her to the land. It's a flat spot with some trees and a small meadow, which would be the perfect spot for a home.

"Not the view, the land, love."

She frowns and looks around. "It's pretty, that's for sure. I like the trees. I'm sorry, what am I missing here?"

I wrap my arm around her shoulders and kiss her temple. "How would you feel about building a home here? With me."

Her head whips around, and she stares up at me in shock, the way she did when I asked her to move in with me.

Was that just a week ago? It feels like a lifetime.

"Seriously? You own this property?"

"If you like it, we'll own it."

Her jaw drops. She takes it all in again and then turns to look out at the ocean.

"I don't see anything here *not* to like, Keegan."

"It won't happen overnight. It'll take time to find the right plans and then actually break ground and build. But it's something I'd love to do with you."

She smiles and leans into me, offering her lips,

which I gladly kiss. "I'm honored and excited. It's gorgeous."

"I'm glad you think so."

"Are you sure you don't want to live in the apartment above the pub, though? Because I don't mind it at all, Keegan. I don't want you to think that I hate it there or something. I'm fine."

"We're fine there for now. But I can't help but look to the future with you, and I want more, Izzy."

"We have time," she assures me and hugs me close. "We have time for all of it."

CHAPTER 16

*O*h my God. What is wrong with me?

I climb into the still-warm bed, burrow under the covers, and will the nausea to go away. I can smell something coming up from the pub. Usually, it would make my mouth water, and I'd go in search of whatever brilliance Fiona was whipping up.

But today, it only makes the nausea worse.

I've been working both jobs for almost two weeks, and the whole time I've felt this way. At first, I blamed it on nerves and exhaustion. My hours are totally messed up, and I don't have a routine.

But now, I think something's wrong.

I reach for my phone and Google my symptoms.

"It has to be the flu," I mutter, reading the small screen. "Except I don't think I have a fever."

I press my hand to my forehead. Nope, no fever.

"I don't have chills. Body aches. Do sore boobs and

hips count? I mean, they're part of my body, so I guess they count. I definitely have the nausea."

Then, I keep reading down the page, and one word hits me in the solar plexus.

Pregnancy.

I sit up and read *those* symptoms.

Nausea.

Breast tenderness.

Smell sensitivity.

That's as far as I get before I toss my phone aside and have to run to the bathroom to dry heave. I have *nothing* left in me.

I sit back on my haunches, still hugging the bowl just in case, and let my mind whirl.

There's no way I can be pregnant. We're always careful. And I just had my period…wait. When did I have a period?

"Oh, shit."

I stand and rinse my mouth out, pull on some clothes, and sneak out the back door of the pub. I drive my little car to the other side of the island, walk into Target, and head for the pharmacy section.

I toss three pregnancy tests and some lip balm into my basket. And then I swing by the bakery for some chocolate chip cookies because I'm going to need them at some point, no matter what the test results are.

If I can stomach the smell of them.

I pay for the goods and hurry back home. Much to my chagrin, Keegan is in the apartment when I walk in.

"Hey, where did you run off to, love?"

"The pharmacy," I say. I don't look him in the eyes, just hurry into the bathroom. "Girl stuff. No worries."

Thank God, I can just say, *"girl stuff."* Men steer clear of those words.

I lock myself in the bathroom and get down to business. I pee on the first stick and set it aside, and then open the cookies.

Yes, it's gross to eat in the bathroom, but I'm suddenly hungry, and these days, I eat when I can.

I'm halfway into the second cookie when I look down at the stick and see two lines.

"What does that mean?" I wonder as I open the instructions and then swallow the now-cardboard bite in my mouth.

Two lines mean I'm pregnant.

"Fuck," I say out loud and drop the stick into the sink.

"Izzy? Are you okay in there?"

"Yeah, I'm fine," I call back and stare at myself in the mirror. "Shit, this is *not* the plan. I don't want him to freak out. I don't want him to think I'm trying to trap him with an anchor baby."

I scrunch up my nose.

"He won't think that. That's dumb."

"Izzy, open the door."

"No, it's okay. I'm fine. You can go."

"You don't sound fine. Let me in."

213

I shake my head and pace the small space. "I just need some time alone."

"Then you shouldn't be with me because that's not what you signed on for here, love. Open up. Let me help."

God, I love him so much, and this is going to change *everything* about our relationship. I don't know if I'm ready for that.

"This sucks," I whisper.

"Okay, last chance, Isabella. I went to get my tools, and I'm about to dismantle this door."

I hear the drill start, and he starts to pull out screws from the hinges.

Finally, I walk over, stick in hand, and unlock the door before he yanks it off.

I pull it open and close my eyes.

But Keegan just wraps his strong arms around me and rocks me back and forth.

"Talk to me, love. There's nothing going on here that we can't figure out. What's wrong?"

I don't speak. I don't pull away. I just wiggle my arm out and raise my hand above my head.

"Is that what I think it is?"

I nod.

"Izzy, it's positive."

"I know," I mumble against his chest.

He picks me up and sits on the couch with me in his lap. "Look at me."

With his finger under my chin, he tips my face up to look at him.

"I know it's *so* early," I say, suddenly unable to keep the words inside. "And unexpected. Trust me, this was *not* my plan. I don't want you to think I'm trying to trap you into staying with me with an anchor baby or anything because I would never do that."

"What in the bleeding hell is an anchor baby?" he asks and brushes my hair over my ear. "Do I look upset to you, Isabella?"

I stop talking and swallow hard, taking in his handsome face. "No."

"There's going to be a lot to think about," he says.

"I know, I just started my new job a couple of weeks ago, and—"

"This isn't 1968, Isabella. They can't fire you because you got pregnant. You can work for as long as you want."

"It's just a *lot* to take in. And I ate a lot of cookies."

"I saw them on the counter."

"You can have one. I'll share."

He laughs and drags his hands up and down my back, soothing me immensely. "We're going to figure this all out, love. First, I think you should probably see a doctor to get it confirmed, and we'll just go from there."

"You make it sound so easy."

"It's not going to be easy." He kisses the top of my head. "But it's simple enough. Don't worry so much."

"I'm going to be sick."

~

"Okay, let's see what we have here," Doctor Simpson says as she squirts gel on a wand and sticks it right up my wazoo.

"Oh, that's not comfortable."

Keegan's hand tightens on mine, and the doctor smiles at me. "Sorry, this won't take too long. Just try to relax. It's more accurate this way, given how early it is in your pregnancy. Okay, so this is the amniotic sack."

I squint, trying to see what she sees as she taps on the screen and places marks around a dark circle.

"And this fluttering, right here, is the baby's heartbeat."

"Well, look at that," Keegan murmurs.

"I don't see a baby," I say, tilting my head.

"You're only about eight weeks along, so it doesn't look like a baby quite yet, but we can see the heart fluttering. It looks strong and perfectly normal for this stage of things."

"You said eight weeks?" I ask, counting back. I've been on the island for about three months. Which means that I got pregnant one of the first times we were together.

And it absolutely, positively can*not* be Troy's.

Thank God.

"Yes, that's what you're measuring here. Does that sound right to you?"

"It's not outside the realm of possibility," Keegan says. "Although, I usually wear a condom."

"Condoms aren't 100% effective," Dr. Simpson reminds him. "Things happen. The good news here is you're healthy, and the baby is healthy."

The baby.

I'm going to have a baby.

She removes the wand and moves away from me. "Do you have any questions before I leave so you can get dressed?"

"Is this horrible nausea normal?" I ask. "I'm sick *all the time.*"

"Unfortunately, yes. It's the change in hormones. I can prescribe something for you if it's too awful. And the good news is, after about twelve weeks, it should start to subside."

"Oh, good, just another month to go."

"You'll need prenatal vitamins, avoid consuming alcohol, cut down on caffeine, and just keep yourself healthy."

"Thank you."

"You're welcome. My nurse will set you up with monthly visits for a while. I'll step out so you can get dressed."

Keegan and I are quiet as I clean myself up and pull on my clothes. The nurse and I schedule the next three-months-worth of appointments, and then Keegan and I walk out to his truck.

But he doesn't start it.

"You don't want this baby," he says quietly. "If that's the way you feel, I wish you'd just say so, Isabella. Because I want to be happy here, and I can't do that when I can see that the situation has you feeling miserable."

I turn to him and feel my eyes fill with tears. "That's not it."

"Hold on." He gets out of the truck and comes around to my side. He somehow manages to get me into his lap in the passenger seat and kisses my cheek.

"I've been sitting in your lap a lot lately. I kind of like it."

"I need you to talk to me, my love."

"I know." I swallow hard and look out the window as I rest my head on his shoulder. "It's not that I don't want children, or even *this* baby. I love babies. When I hold little Thomas, my ovaries ache. Which is silly, but it's a thing. It's just…this wasn't on my radar at all for a while. It's such a surprise, and I wasn't ready. And this part is going to sound so selfish, I'm ashamed of myself."

"You're not selfish at all, Isabella. And you can say anything at all to me. What is it?"

"I thought we'd have a few years alone first. To build our house, and our life, and get to know each other better. And now we won't have that, and it makes me sad."

"That doesn't sound selfish at all. Not to me."

I kiss his cheek and wipe a tear from my face.

"It's taken us both by surprise, and that's the truth of it, love. But children are blessings, no matter when they decide to make their grand entrance. We still have time to do all of the things you mentioned. And once the baby is here, we'll continue to do those things with him in tow."

"What if it's a her?"

He grins and kisses my head. "With her in tow, then."

I take a deep breath and let it out slowly. "I know you're right. I know that everything is going to work out, and we'll find our footing. It's just a little scary."

"Of course, it is."

"Is it scary for you, too?"

"I'm scared out of my mind, truth be told."

"You're so calm."

"There's no need to freak out. Because, like you said, we'll find our footing. We have a lot of people around to help. There's a lot of love to go around, you know?"

"I know, and it makes me so happy. Your family has made me feel welcome from the first day I got here. I love them all so much."

"And they love you. My parents are going to jump for joy when we tell them."

"Can you do me a favor?" I ask.

"Anything."

"Can we wait to tell everyone else? Just for a little while. Most couples wait until they're about twelve weeks along, just to be sure that everything's okay."

"That's another month, Izzy."

"I know. And I probably won't need that long. I just have to wrap my head around everything. Give me just a couple of weeks?"

"I can do that." He kisses my head again and then tips my chin up to cover my lips with his. "I love you so much, Isabella."

"I love you, too." I feel my lip quiver as he drags his fingertips down my cheek. "Thank you for not assuming this is an anchor baby."

"What does that mean, exactly?"

"You know, when a girl gets pregnant on purpose, so the guy has to stay with her. Or so she thinks."

"That's the most ridiculous thing I've ever heard."

"I know, it's dumb. And I wouldn't do that."

"Of course, you wouldn't. I think I need to remind you that loving someone means you assume the best of them, not the worst. I wouldn't jump to horrible conclusions when something unexpected happens in our lives. And I would hope you wouldn't, either."

"The people I've had in my life before would, Keegan. And it's sometimes hard to rewire the way you think. But I'm working on it. And I'm grateful for you and your steady calm. I'm sorry that you thought I wasn't happy about this."

"I wondered if you wanted to end the pregnancy."

I turn wide eyes up to him. "No, I don't want to do that. I don't *need* to do that. I just need some time to get used to the idea, that's all."

"Like I said, we have time. She's not coming next week."

"What if it's a he?"

He laughs and hugs me to him. "You're funny, you know that? He's not coming next week. Nothing is happening right away."

"And that's good because I don't have the energy to handle anything else right now. I'm tired all the time and can't stop throwing up."

"Do you need the night off? You can get some rest, and I'll call Maeve into work. Her hand is all healed up. She's right as rain."

"No, I can work. Besides, it's a Wednesday, it won't be too busy. The weekends are hard because I work late into the night the rest of the week, but when I go to the other job, it's super early in the morning. My internal clock is confused."

"I bet. From now on, you won't work Thursday nights so you have that and Friday to go to bed earlier."

"That'll help," I concede. "I can work earlier in the day, just a short shift for the lunch crowd so Maggie isn't there for so long."

"That should work." He nuzzles my temple. "Are we okay, then?"

"Yeah, we're good. I feel better after talking it all through. Everything's going to work out just fine."

"It's going to be bloody brilliant," he replies. "Now, let's get home so you can get a nap before work, yeah?"

"You read my mind. I also want chocolate chip cookies."

"That's all you've eaten over the past few days."

"I know, it's the only thing that sounds good, and the only thing that doesn't come right back up again. I tried eating your mom's stew last night because it's always my favorite, but I couldn't stomach it."

"Well, then chocolate chip cookies it is for now. As long as you're eating something. And we'll pick up some vitamins for you."

"And chocolate milk."

He looks down at me in surprise. "The baby wants chocolate milk."

He laughs and shakes his head. "Then the wee one will have it."

CHAPTER 17

I'm just so tired. I could sleep standing up. Or anywhere, really. It's been a week since I saw the doctor, and the symptoms are no better. I'm exhausted, can't keep much down, and holy shit, do my boobs hurt.

But I'm starting to get a little more excited. I downloaded the book *What to Expect When You're Expecting* onto my iPad the other night and started reading it. And in the morning, after I woke up, I lay in bed for a bit to look at baby room ideas.

Now that I know that Keegan isn't only okay with the idea but also excited, I'm getting used to it all.

I still don't want to say anything to anyone else for a little while, just to make sure nothing horrible happens.

It's Friday afternoon, and I'm covering the lunch crowd at the pub so I can go upstairs early and get some sleep before I have to make the trip into Seattle to report the weather in the morning. The schedule is brutal, but I love the job so much that I don't mind.

"It's slow today," I say as I set my empty tray on the bar and boost my ass into a stool.

"That it is," Keegan says as he washes a beer glass. "Take a second to get off your feet, why don't you?"

"Already doing it."

When it's just Keegan and me in the pub like this, I don't have to work so hard to pretend that everything's normal. Not that I'm a whiner, I just take more little breaks to sit and breathe, usually working my way through a wave of nausea.

But right now, it's just exhaustion.

I rest my head on my arm and close my eyes for a moment. I can hear everything around me, but I'm in a nice, drifty place.

"Go up and go to bed," Keegan says softly. "I can handle the bar until Maggie gets here in just a little while."

"No, I'm fine." I sit up and prop my chin on my hand. "I'm sorry, this is incredibly unprofessional. Please don't fire me."

He grins at me, and I can't help but smile back. This man's smile is *everything*. He can boost me up with just a wink, a simple *look.*

Is it any wonder that I fell in love with him?

"Okay, back to work." I hop off the stool, but a wave of nausea hits me so fast and hard that I have to make a run for the bathroom.

When is this going to stop? I ask myself as I stand at the sink and rinse my mouth out. I've lost five pounds in the past week.

This can't be healthy. I'm going to have to call the doctor for the meds she mentioned at our appointment. I thought I could stick it out, but something has to give here.

Just as I open the door to step out into the bar area, Maggie appears and gently pushes me back into the bathroom.

"What are you doing here early?" I ask her.

"I came to see Ma for a minute before my shift starts. But we don't want to talk about me. You're pregnant, aren't you?"

"How did—? No. Of course, not. I don't know what you're talking about, Mary Margaret."

"Don't you *Mary Margaret* me, Isabella. I'm not blind or stupid. You look exhausted all the time, and this isn't the first time I've seen you make a run for the bathroom. Either you have an eating disorder, which I highly doubt, or you have a bun in the oven."

I sigh and lean against the wall. I cross my arms over my chest and feel the soreness in my boobs.

Maybe I do need to talk to someone besides Keegan about this. A woman.

A *friend.*

"First of all, you can't tell a *soul.*"

"I knew it." She does a little happy dance right in the middle of the restroom. "I *knew* it."

"I'm serious. We aren't telling anyone for a little bit to make sure that everything goes right, and the baby's healthy. It's still super early."

"I can totally keep a secret," she says, but I know better.

"If you tell anyone, you won't be my favorite anymore."

The smile leaves her face. "Well, that's just mean."

"I'm not joking."

"But you *are* pregnant."

"Or I've had the flu for several weeks." I grin. "We went to the doctor. We saw the heartbeat and everything."

"Oh my God, this is so exciting! Another little baby to love on. I'm so excited for you, Izzy. Keegan must be over the moon. Wait, is he the one who doesn't want to say anything? Because now that I think about it, I don't know that kids were ever on his radar."

"No, it's me. Keegan's really excited."

"You're so good for my brother," she says, and the words instantly bring tears of joy to my eyes. "I've seen so much of him come alive since you came into his life, Izzy. He's happier. So, thanks for that."

"Well, it's mutual. I love him very much."

Maggie squeals and wraps her arms around me in a big hug. "Do you need anything?"

"I need to stop throwing up."

"Crackers," she says. "Stasia was this way. You need crackers, and maybe some chicken broth. And you should suck on hard ginger candies. Ginger is good for nausea. We have ginger ale at the bar, we'll get you set up."

"If I'd known I would get so much good advice, I would have said something earlier. Keegan knows nothing about this stuff. And neither do I. I've never really been around a pregnant woman."

"Don't worry, we know what to do."

I'VE BEEN SUCKING on ginger candies and eating crackers for twenty-four hours, and I already feel better. Maybe it was a mistake to not say anything to at least the other girls. I didn't consider that they'd have so much good advice for me.

"Great job this morning, Izzy," my boss, Roger, says as he approaches my desk. "I have to say, you've exceeded our expectations these past few weeks. Congratulations."

I sit back in my chair and smile at the man I've come to respect since I started working for the news program. "Thank you. I'm so happy to hear that you're pleased with my work."

"We are. Listen, you just reported about the ice storm that's likely to hit Portland tomorrow afternoon."

"That's right. If the models are correct, and they usually are, it should rain heavily all morning, and then start to freeze in the early afternoon. It's one of those odd storms that rolls in during the fall sometimes."

"I'm sending you down to cover it remotely for the evening news."

I sit back and stare at the man. This is *amazing*. "Really?"

"Yes. Really. You'll be on location, reporting back live to the anchors in the studio for the five o'clock and six o'clock news."

"Okay." I tap my chin, thinking of everything I have to get ready.

"Is there a problem?"

"Not at all. I'm making a mental list of everything I have to do. When will we leave? Will we be gone overnight?"

"I would plan for that in case the weather is so bad that you get stuck there. You'll be just a team of two, you and Phil, who will drive and man the camera. He's a veteran at this. Been here for twenty years."

"I met Phil, he's very nice. Okay, so what time will we leave?"

"Eleven in the morning to make sure you get there safely before the ice hits."

I nod, and Roger walks away.

This whole job is my dream, but *this* part, going on location and reporting the weather as it happens, is something I've always wanted to do.

I don't care if it's in the middle of a blizzard, a

hurricane, or an ice storm, it sounds like a lot of fun to me.

And now I'm being given the opportunity to do it. I take a deep breath and start to shut down my laptop so I can make my way home and give Keegan the good news. He'll have to give me tomorrow night off from the pub, but that shouldn't be a problem.

Because it's the middle of the morning on a Saturday, the traffic isn't too bad, and the ferry makes good time across the Sound to our little island. The pub isn't far from the dock, and I'm all smiles when I walk into the apartment.

Keegan is just pouring a cup of coffee.

I don't say anything at all, just hurry over to him, grip his shirt in my fist, and pull him down for a long, passionate kiss.

"Someone feels better," he murmurs when I pull back.

"I do feel better today. Maggie figured it out, the pregnancy, and she suggested ginger and crackers. It's helped a lot."

"She didn't even say anything to me."

"I threatened that she wouldn't be my favorite anymore if she blabbed." I laugh at the stunned look on his face. "Seems it worked."

"I wish I'd known that's all it took all these years. But I thought *I* was your favorite."

"We won't tell her." I wink and then do a little happy dance. "I have good news."

"Tell me everything. You were brilliant this morning, by the way. That blue pantsuit is gorgeous on you."

"Thanks, I found it at the Rack for forty dollars. Anyway, I'm going to need tomorrow night off here at the pub because my boss is sending me down to Portland to report on location. Isn't that *amazing?*"

"Based on how excited you are right now, I'm going to say, yes. It's amazing."

"I've always wanted to report from the field as the weather happens. Always, Keegan. And they're sending me. Roger said I'm doing a good job."

"Of course, he did. I have eyes in my head, don't I? Even I can see that you're fantastic at what you do. And I'm so proud of you. But I also want to make sure you're safe, so give me the details."

I smile up at him, expecting nothing less.

"A very nice man named Phil will be driving us down in the storm chaser van. The *storm chaser* van, Keegan. Isn't that cool?"

He laughs and nods, and I keep going.

"Anyway, he's been doing the job for more than twenty years. I've met him, and he's very nice. He'll also be manning the camera. So it'll just be the two of us. We leave late in the morning tomorrow, and I have to plan to stay in Portland for the night, depending on the weather, of course."

"That makes sense."

"I'm going to be reporting live for the evening news. The *evening* news."

"I'll have every TV in the pub tuned in and be sure to hush everyone so we can listen."

I walk into his arms and hug him tightly and then let my hands roam down his back to his ass, currently covered by only basketball shorts.

"Can I entice you back to bed for a while?" I ask as he sets his mug aside and lowers his lips to mine.

"No enticing needed, love." His hands immediately get to work on my clothes, leaving a trail of apparel from the kitchen to the bedroom. I push his shorts over his hips and take his heavy length in my hand.

I've been too sick to make love with him over the past couple of weeks.

But today, I feel great.

And I've missed him.

"I want to attack you," I confess as my hands wander over his nakedness. "But I also want to take it kind of slow because it's been a minute and I..."

"You what, Isabella?"

I bite my lip and drag my fingertips up to his shoulders. "I missed you."

"Ah, baby." The kiss is gentle as he leads me back onto the bed. He covers me, buries his hands in my hair and takes his time kissing me thoroughly. Those magical lips tease me. His tongue excites me.

And when his mouth wanders away from mine to make its way down my neck, over my collarbone, and to my breast, I sigh in relief.

"Are they tender?" he asks.

"A little." Okay, a lot, but right now, everything he does feels amazing.

He's careful as he kisses and licks a nipple, then pays the same attention to the other side.

He presses wet kisses down my torso to my still-mostly-flat belly and nuzzles it with his nose as if to say "*hello*" to the sleeping baby inside.

It's incredibly sweet and sexy at the same time.

The apartment is quiet but for our sighs of pleasure, and our moans of delight as we tumble across the bed.

CHAPTER 18

~KEEGAN~

I don't think I'll ever get enough of this woman. Just when I think I know everything, when I've *felt* everything there is to feel, she surprises me.

Her leg climbs higher around my hip as she opens herself in invitation.

She doesn't have to ask twice. Not today or any other day.

I link my fingers with hers and slowly slide inside. Christ, she fits me like a fucking glove.

"You're incredible," I whisper against her lips. "Gorgeous. Sassy."

Her lips tip up in a grin, and then she groans when I grind myself against her, pressed as deep as I can go.

"Go faster," she pleads.

"No." I nibble her lips lazily, enjoying her. "We're going to enjoy ourselves for a while."

"Oh, trust me, I'm enjoying it." She tightens around me, and I see stars. "Just go a little faster."

I can't resist her. I pick up the pace just a bit and watch as she arches her back in pleasure, her cheeks and chest flushed with desire.

She's everything I've ever wanted in this world.

I take her higher and watch with amazement as she tumbles over into the first orgasm. She clenches around me, her nails digging into my arms as she holds on for dear life.

And when that one subsides, I go even faster, a touch harder, and watch as her mouth opens, and she moans in delight.

"Oh my God, Keegan."

"That's right, love. Give me more."

"I can't."

I smile down at her. "You can."

She shakes her head against the pillow, but when I reach between us and plant my fingertip against her already swollen clit, she cries out and comes spectacularly. The pressure building at the base of my spine erupts, and I fall over with her into paradise.

As soon as I can breathe again, I roll to the side and cradle Izzy to me.

"Good morning, my love."

She smiles and lets out a little laugh. "This is the best morning I've had in a long while."

"I think you should nap for a bit," I suggest. "Get some rest for a bit and recharge."

"You should nap with me," she says on a yawn. "Also, can I just say that I'm so happy the nausea is starting to get better? Who knew ginger would help?"

"I guess people do drink ginger ale when they're sick," I say.

"I've never heard of that," she replies. "My nanny always gave me Sprite."

"Did it help?" I brush the hair off her face as she nuzzles against the pillow to fall asleep.

"I don't remember. I don't get sick very often."

I lean in and kiss her nose. "It's glad I am that you're feeling better. It's a helpless feeling to watch you suffer. I'd gladly take it away, take it on myself if I could."

"No, men are babies when they're sick. I'd rather just deal."

I laugh and kiss her again. "Sleep."

"Are you going to nap with me?"

"I'll be nearby." I should do any number of things down in the pub, but it's covered for now, and there's no reason I can't spend some time up here with Izzy. "I'll be right here."

"Okay." Her voice is soft, and her face is that of an angel as she drifts off to sleep.

I've never loved anyone more than I do the woman lying next to me.

"Just look at our girl on the television," Frank says from his stool at the bar. "She's a pretty sight, and that's the truth."

"That she is, my friend." I turn to look at her and smile. She's standing on a residential street, bundled up in a black coat with the station's logo on the chest, a hat, and gloves.

"As you can see, the rain from just a few hours ago has turned to pure ice. It coats the trees, the power-lines, and most definitely the streets. Officials are asking everyone to stay inside as much as possible and off the roads. This could certainly turn deadly very quickly."

The screen shifts to the anchors in the studio, and I get back to work.

"Izzy might be the coolest person I know," Maeve says. "And I know some *very* cool people."

"I couldn't agree more, but I'm just a smidge biased." I laugh as I set two pints of Guinness on Maeve's tray.

"How early did she have to leave this morning?" Shawn asks as he walks out of the kitchen to fill up his water bottle.

The entire family is here, just like they were at Kane's on Izzy's first day of work. Shawn, Lexi, and Ma have been in and out of the kitchen to keep an eye on the TV, and I finally called a halt to food service until after the last part of the news so everyone could watch.

No one complained.

"Around eight, I guess. She wanted to have plenty of

time to prepare at the office before they drove down. And it's good that she did because they got down there just as the cold weather set in. She'll probably be there overnight."

"It's probably for the best," Shawn says. "I wouldn't want to drive in that. It's crazy how the weather is. It's dry as a bone and sunny outside here, yet she's in an ice storm just a few hours away."

"You know what they say," Frank adds, "if you don't like the weather in the Pacific Northwest, just hang out for ten minutes because it'll change. Reminds me of my beloved Ireland."

"Oh, she's coming back on," Maggie says, pointing to the TV. "Turn it up, Keegan."

The whole pub hushes as Izzy starts to speak.

"I'm back live, and we decided to drive around a bit to give you a better look at what's happening around us. I have the window rolled down because we can hear the limbs on the trees breaking along the street as we drive."

"Oh, darlin', be careful," Da murmurs from beside me.

"If you listen carefully, you can hear the popping," she continues. "But what's incredibly fascinating to me is the speed at which this happened. It honestly looked like Elsa threw up her hands, and everything suddenly froze. Look at that sheet of ice on the road before us."

They're traveling on a bridge extending over the interstate.

"There are very few cars below us on the freeway, but...oh my goodness, look! That car is skidding, clearly going way too fast. And whoa, you guys, he's now spinning in a complete circle. Oh, God!"

Before our eyes, the van she's traveling in begins sliding out of control. Izzy shrieks, and the man driving yells, *"Hold on!"* as they suddenly hit the guardrail.

The feed goes black. Everyone in the pub gasps.

"Oh my, it looks like the storm chaser van just got into a bit of trouble, but don't worry, folks, I'm sure they're just fine."

"What just fucking happened?" I demand, staring at the TV. "Did she just fall over to the freeway below?"

"No." Shawn's still standing next to me, cool and calm. "No, the guardrail stopped them. They weren't going that fast."

"The rail fell," Maggie says, her eyes wide. "Didn't you see it before it went dark? The rail fell, and it looked like—"

"Stop talking," Kane says, wrapping his arm around her shoulders. "Izzy is perfectly fine."

"Of course, she is," Maggie agrees.

But I saw it, too. "She went over."

I reach for my phone and immediately dial her number. It goes to voicemail.

"I can't reach her."

"It's been *seconds*," Da reminds me. "Give it a beat. Look, they're coming back on."

"Welcome back to news at six. We are still trying to make contact with Izzy in the storm chaser van. We're not sure what the status is, but we have emergency personnel on the way to their location. We will update you when we have more information."

"Such a scary situation, Bob, and proof of just how dangerous it is down there right now. If you're in Portland tonight, hunker down and stay safe."

"I need to get to her." I pace behind the bar. "Who do we know with a private plane? Luke?"

"You can't go down there in the storm," Shawn says. "Keegan, she's going to be just fine. We'll know more in a few minutes. I'll bet she calls any second."

"She's pregnant," I blurt out. "It's *both* of them that I'm worried about."

"I didn't tell," Maggie announces. "For the record, it came from him."

"She's pregnant?" Ma asks and clutches her hands at her breast. "Oh, darling, this is wonderful news."

The pub erupts with chatter and gasps of joy.

"Does this mean I can't marry her, then?" Frank asks, making me smile for the first time.

"It does. I'll be marrying her myself if I can get her home safely. Damn it, why won't she answer the bloody phone?"

"Because it's probably not nearby," Kane says. "I never answer my phone, and I'm perfectly fine."

"Something we're working on," Stasia says, rolling her eyes.

"And we're back with information," Bob says on the television. "As you can see, we're using the live feed from our sister station in Portland. From their vantage point on the freeway below, it looks like the van is hanging precariously over the side of the overpass."

"Fuck me," I say and rub my hand over my lips. The woman I love more than life itself is hanging off the side of an overpass in an ice storm. My stomach climbs into my throat, and my bowels turn to liquid.

I'm going to be sick.

"We can't see inside the van, but as you can see, fire trucks are arriving to help as we speak."

"They didn't fall," Da says and pats my shoulder. "She's okay."

"The front of the van is smashed," I reply. "She could be hurt."

Lights flash on the screen as the men in the trucks jump into action.

I've never been so scared in my life.

"I feel so damn helpless. I'm just *standing* here."

"There's nothing else you can do," Cameron says. He's been quietly watching the screen from his perch on a stool. The pub is perfectly quiet as we watch it all unfold.

Then the screen changes back to the studio.

"We think it's best to come back to the studio in case the families are watching this and something goes wrong. But don't worry, we'll keep you posted as we learn more."

"Damn it!"

"Hey." Da cups my face in his hands. "She's safe right now, and that's what you need to keep reminding yourself. Right this minute, she's safe. Dozens of people are there right now to help her."

"But *I'm* not there."

"And you can't do anything about that, son. So, you need to trust in those professionals—and in Izzy to keep a straight head. She's a smart woman, our girl, and she's going to be back on solid ground in just a few moments."

I nod and take a deep breath. He's right, losing my shit won't change this or make it better.

But, damn it, I want to get to her and pull her into my arms to make sure she's okay.

"When were you going to tell us that you're having a baby?" Maeve asks.

"In a couple of weeks." I turn to her. "Isabella wanted to make sure everything was okay before we told everyone, just in case."

"We did that," Stasia says. "It's understandable. And she and the baby are going to be great."

I nod and turn back to the TV, hoping they'll show me the van again. Or better yet, Izzy herself.

She has to be okay. There is no other option.

CHAPTER 19

"*A*re you okay?"

I can't speak. I can only stare down the front end of the van to the freeway below.

"Izzy, are you okay?"

"I don't know."

"Oh my God," Phil says next to me. We're both perfectly still. "I don't know if we're teetering or if we're hung up on the guardrail."

"It's icy." I swallow hard. "We could slip off."

I hear him take a long, deep breath. I'm doing my best not to freak the hell out. My heart is hammering, my blood rushing through my ears.

I feel sick, and it has nothing at all to do with the pregnancy.

"I'm pregnant," I blurt. "Not how I planned to tell anyone, but here we are."

"Okay, I need you to listen to me, Izzy. Are you listening?"

"Yes. But speak up because it's hard to hear past the roaring in my head."

"We're going to make it out of here just fine. You and the baby are both good. Did you hit your head or anything when we hit the guardrail?"

"No. Why didn't the airbag go off?"

"Good question. The station knows what happened. We were on-air. They've called in help by now."

"Okay." I lick my lips. "That makes me feel a little better. And I hear sirens. You've been doing this for a long time. Has this happened before?"

"I wouldn't still be doing this if it had happened before."

"Great."

"You did great at cutting off the camera when it all happened."

"I didn't want Keegan to see it. That's what flashed through my head; that if I died today, I didn't want that in his head for the rest of his life."

"We're not dying today. Tomorrow is my wife's forty-fifth birthday, and I have reservations at her favorite place. We're finally empty nesters after having kids in the house for more than twenty years. I'm going to enjoy the next forty years with my wife. And you're going to have that baby and live another eighty years yourself."

"Right." I take a deep breath. "Sure. Tell her I said happy birthday, by the way."

The van slips, just a few inches, but it feels like feet. I scream.

"Okay, this isn't fun," Phil says.

A fire truck pulls in behind us. I see two more in my peripheral vision.

"People are here. Thank God."

It feels like forever before I hear someone on a loudspeaker say, "Open your window."

I do as he asks, by just barely moving my arm to press on the button. I don't want to move too much in case it causes us to fall.

"I want you to know that you're not going to fall. You're hung up on the guardrail. But we have to figure out how we're going to tow you back onto the road in this ice. It might be a while before we get you out of there. Your doors are too far over the edge. The tires are off the pavement. But I repeat, you're not in danger of falling."

"Thank Christ," Phil mutters.

I reach my arm out the window and give the man a thumbs-up, then roll the window back up because it's damn cold outside.

"All I've ever wanted is to do on-scene reporting for the weather. And look where that got me—hanging over the side of an overpass."

"It doesn't usually happen like this, you know."

"But why is it my luck that it happened this time?"

Phil shrugs. "If it happens to us once in our careers, you got it over with in the beginning. It'll be boring from here on out."

"I hope you're right because I don't want to do this again."

We hear and feel the team working behind us as they hitch something to the back of the van—at least that's what I assume they're doing. But when the fire truck starts to pull us back, the tires only spin out on the ice.

"They have to use some ice melt under their tires," Phil mutters.

"I think I see them grabbing buckets of something," I reply, watching in the side mirror. "I wish I could call Keegan and tell him what's happening, but my phone is in my bag in the back. Do you have your phone?"

"It's in the back, too," Phil says. "We only had a half a mile to go before we planned to pull over again."

"Yeah." I sigh and watch in the mirror as they try again to pull us back. This time, the truck gets traction, and the metal of the van screeches as we scrape along the broken guardrail.

When we're back on the road, I break down into tears.

Our doors are yanked open simultaneously as firefighters help us from the van.

"Are you hurt?" a woman asks, looking me over. "The airbags didn't go off."

"No, but I'm okay, I think. I didn't hit my head. I'm pregnant, though. About ten weeks along."

"We have to go to the hospital," Phil says. "It's company policy to go get checked out if something like this happens."

"The ambulance is over here," my firefighter says.

"I need my phone."

"We'll get it out of the van and bring it to you," she assures me. "The ambulance is waiting."

I'm rushed into the back of the ambulance, and I'm frustrated. I want to call Keegan. I know he must be worried out of his mind.

When we're on the road, I look at the EMT. "Can I borrow your phone to call my boyfriend so he knows I'm okay? We were on live TV."

"Sure. What's the number?"

I stop and stare at him. "Uh, can you Google it? He's at the pub. O'Callaghan's Pub."

He taps on his screen and then turns it to me. "This one?"

"Yes."

He taps again and then passes me the phone. I press it to my ear and only listen to it ring once before Keegan answers.

"O'Callaghan's."

"It's me. Oh my God, Keegan, it was so damn scary. I can't believe we slid right over the side of the road. And I didn't have my phone because it was in the back, and it took the firefighters forever to pull us back onto the road."

"Stop. Are you okay? Did you fall to the freeway below?"

"No. I mean, yes."

"Which is it?"

"Yes, I'm okay. And no, we didn't fall. The van got hung up on the guardrail."

"Thank Christ. She's all right!"

"Who's there?"

"Everyone. I've been worried sick, love. You're sure you're okay?"

"I think so. We're being taken to Emanuel hospital to be checked out, just to be sure. I don't want to stay the night here, but I might have to, especially since the van is wrecked. But I'll keep you posted."

"I'll come get you."

I hold the phone tighter, wishing with all my might it were that easy. "No, the roads are too bad down here, Keegan. I won't risk you. I'll keep you posted. I should have my phone soon, and then I can keep you updated better."

"I'm just glad to hear your voice and know that you're safe. I swear, I lost ten years off my life."

"Me, too. I'll call you soon. I love you."

"I love you, Isabella."

I hang up and pass the EMT his phone. "Thank you."

He nods, slips the phone into his pocket, and

continues monitoring my vital signs. When we reach the hospital, they take Phil and me to different rooms.

A doctor hurries in and smiles at me. "I saw that happen in real-time. Scared the hell out of me."

"You and me both. I'm ten weeks pregnant."

"Did you hit your head?"

How many times am I going to be asked that? "No."

He feels around my neck. "You could have a bit of whiplash. And you have some bruising from the seatbelt."

"I do?" I glance down and see the black and blue marks on my right shoulder. "Oh, wow."

"That's pretty standard for something like this. Are you cramping at all?"

"No."

"I'm going to have you use the restroom so we know if you're spotting. I doubt the baby is hurt at all, but we want to make sure."

I nod and walk down the hallway to the restroom. I'm relieved that there's no blood on the toilet paper.

When I go back to the room, Phil's already in there.

"They let you go so soon?" I ask as I sit on the bed.

"Yeah, there's nothing wrong with me," he says with a smile. "Just shook up, is all. How are you feeling?"

"I'm bruised, but overall, not too bad. I'll probably be sore tomorrow."

"You and me both. We're going back tonight, by the way. The station is sending the helicopter for us."

"Oh, God, I have to ride in a helicopter in an ice storm?"

"It's letting up now," he says. "It's moving south. Seattle didn't get anything at all. This one wasn't so bad. Aside from the whole near-death experience thing."

"Well, good. Because I want to go home."

"Me, too."

THEY WOULDN'T LET me drive home. When we got back to the studio, we had to answer some questions, and then Roger gave me a ride home—even though it was two hours out of his way.

"I could have driven," I say for the fiftieth time when he drives his Lexus SUV off the ferry.

"No," he says. "You're shaken up, and your commute is brutal enough as it is. We'll get your car to you in the next day or so."

"Thank you."

"You're welcome." He pulls up at the front of the pub. "Here you are. If you need anything at all before we see you on Saturday, just let us know. I'm serious, Izzy."

"I will." I smile over at him. "Thanks for being so nice today."

"You had a hell of a day," he says. "And I'm responsible for you. I'm just relieved that you and Phil are safe and healthy."

"Me, too." I open the door and reach for my purse. "I'll see you on Saturday."

He waves, and I walk inside, surprised to find so many family members sitting in the pub. The mood is subdued, which isn't unusual for a Sunday night, but it feels even more somber tonight.

It's almost midnight. So much has happened in the past twelve hours, it boggles my mind.

"Izzy!" Maggie exclaims and runs over to hug me close. "Oh, thank God."

I hug her back as the rest of the family descends on me, passing me around for hugs and kisses on the cheek.

Keegan pulls me close at last, and I lose it. The tears I've held in check all day start to tumble out of my eyes.

His strong hands rub up and down my back, and then he simply picks me up and sets me down on a chair. He doesn't leave me. He holds me as I have a good cry. I hear people talking and moving about, but all I can do is sob.

"Ah, lass, you're breaking my heart."

That's Frank's voice. It makes me smile and cry at the same time.

These people are my family. All of them. Even Frank.

Finally, I pull back and accept an offered wad of tissues to dab at my eyes.

"I'm sorry I'm such a mess."

"You had an emotional day," Tom says kindly. "Of course, you have some tears to get out."

"And hormones will do it, as well," Fiona says.

I look up at Keegan in surprise.

"I didn't tell," Maggie says from somewhere behind Keegan. "I'm still the favorite."

"It slipped out," Keegan says, speaking for the first time, really. "I was freaking out a bit, love."

"It's okay." I wipe another tear. "For just a moment, I thought I wouldn't see you again. It's why I turned the camera off as soon as we started going over. Because if I was going to die, I didn't want you to watch it."

"You are *not* going to die." His voice is fierce as he cups my face. "I thought my heart might fall out of my chest when I saw it happening."

"I don't ever want to relive it."

"You're bruised," he says, looking down to where my sweater has slipped to the side. "Is the baby okay?"

"We're both fine. I'll probably be a little sore for a couple of days, but it's just some bruises, thank goodness. Phil is fine, too. We were lucky."

He hugs me close again, relief radiating from him. "Thank God, you're home."

"I was so happy when Phil said we weren't staying. I just wanted to see you. To see all of you."

"Isabella," Keegan says and clears his throat. "I want you to marry me."

I stare up at him in shock. "Why do you always ask me these things when I least expect them?"

"I'm not asking."

"Well, you should be," someone calls out, making us both laugh.

"You're right." He lowers to one knee, and the room goes so quiet, you could hear a pin drop. "Isabella Harris, marry me. If today taught me anything at all, it's that life is too precious, too valuable, to wait. I love you, and I know that love won't ever go away. I want you with me always. To raise our children and build our life together."

"Still didn't ask," Kane says.

"Will you marry me, then?"

I lean in and press my lips to his. "Yes. I'll marry you, Keegan O'Callaghan."

"We have so much to celebrate," Fiona says as she wipes a tear from her eye. "Babies and weddings. Two of my favorite things."

"I love you," Keegan whispers to me. "Let's do it next week."

I laugh out loud and then shrug. "I'll find us the best weather day, and we'll go from there."

EPILOGUE

~IZZY~

"*H*ow did we do this in six days?" I wonder aloud as Fiona fusses with my veil. I'm in a guest bedroom suite at Kane's house, getting dressed for my wedding day. Soon, in just a few minutes, someone will drive me over to the ceremony site where Keegan and I plan to build our home.

"You had a fleet of women at your disposal, that's how," Fiona says as she steps back and looks me over with a critical eye. "You're a beautiful bride, Izzy."

I turn to the full-length mirror and smile. The dress is perfect. And better yet, I picked it out. Not my mother. Or even my father, for that matter.

Everything about today is exactly the way Keegan and I want it to be.

"I'm sorry that your mother isn't here," Fiona says and stands next to me, looking at me in the mirror.

"I'm not." I take her hand and hold it tightly. "She

and my dad were invited, and they declined. They've made it clear how they feel. And, honestly, Fiona, I'm okay with it. You've been more of a mother to me in the past few months than my mom ever was. It should be you here helping me get ready to marry your son."

"I wasn't going to cry," she says and dabs at her eye. "At least, not yet. But I'm just so happy for my boy. He found the perfect young woman for him, and it makes a mother's heart soar to see her son so happy."

"Well, thank you for raising such a good man."

"You guys being mushy in here?" Maggie asks as she and Maeve walk inside. "Everyone's over at the ceremony site, ready to go when you are, Izzy."

"Oh, I'm ready." I grab my bouquet and take a deep breath, relieved when I don't feel like throwing up.

It seems I am getting past the worst of the morning sickness.

"Let's do this, shall we?" The four of us walk down the stairs to the little ATV that's waiting to give us a ride. When we get there, we're laughing from how bumpy the ride was. Maeve, Maggie, and Fiona all give me hugs before they go find their seats.

"Thank you for walking me down the aisle." I kiss Tom on the cheek and am delighted when he blushes.

"It's an honor and a privilege, Izzy, my girl. Now, are you sure this is what you want to do? My Keegan is a fine boy, but he's a stubborn one, as well."

"Well, I can be stubborn myself. Yes, of course, this is what I want."

"Good." The music starts, and he pats my hand after I loop it through his arm.

As far as the weather goes, today was the best day. It's partly cloudy with just the touch of a light breeze— and a one hundred percent chance of love.

As I walk down the aisle, I don't see all of our closest friends and family around us, including the entire Montgomery family and their children. I don't see the beautiful flowers and the arbor we managed to set up in record time. I don't even hear the rush of the ocean behind us.

I only have eyes for one man.

Keegan's eyes latch on to mine, and then they grow misty as he takes me in from head to toe. Every woman wants her groom to look at her just like this on their wedding day, and I'm not disappointed.

This, right here, is what I deserve. It's what I need. And I didn't find it in a stuffy church in Salem, Oregon, but rather on a little island in the Pacific Ocean with a handsome, wonderful Irishman.

"Okay, everybody, gather around! Single ladies!" I call out to all of the girls, and they form a half-circle behind me.

"Maeve, get a move on," Maggie says, gesturing to her sister.

"What are we doing?" Maeve asks.

"Okay, get ready," I say as I spin and then toss a smaller version of my bouquet over my shoulder. When I turn around again, I see that Maeve caught it.

"What in the hell?" she demands. "No. I didn't sign up for this."

"You came over here of your own free will," Maggie says.

"I thought we were getting more cake. I don't want this. I'm not getting married next. Here, Mary Margaret, you take it."

"Nope, you caught it."

Maeve turns to me. "Catch!"

She tosses it back to me, but I just laugh and immediately throw it back to her. "It's yours now, whether you like it or not."

"Well, shit."

ARE you excited for Maeve O'Callaghan's love story! It's coming this year, in Flirt With Me! You can read all about it, and find preorder links, here: https://www. kristenprobyauthor.com/flirtwithme

AND DON'T FORGET, With Me In Seattle MAFIA is just around the corner! Click here for more info: https:// www.kristenprobyauthor.com/underboss

WITH ME IN SEATTLE CHARACTER GLOSSARY

With more than twenty stories in the With Me In Seattle Series, I figured it was time to include a who's who in the world, listed by family. Please know this may contain spoilers for anyone who hasn't read all of the books, but it's a great reference for those who want to make sure they read about everyone.

The Williams Family

Luke Williams – Hollywood movie producer. Married to Natalie Williams, a professional photographer. Parents to Olivia, Keaton, Haley and Chelsea. {Come Away With Me}

Samantha Williams Nash – Professional. Married to mega rock star Leo Nash. {Rock With Me}

Mark Williams – Works in Construction, for Isaac Montgomery. Married to professional dancer

Meredith Summers. Parents to Lucy and Hudson. {Breathe With Me}

The Montgomery Family

Steven and Gail Montgomery – Parents of Isaac, Matt, Caleb, Will and Jules. Steven is the father of Dominic.

Isaac Montgomery – Eldest sibling. Owner for Montgomery Construction. Married to stay at home mom Stacy Montgomery. Parents to Sophie and Liam. {Under the Mistletoe With Me}

Matt Montgomery – Detective with the Seattle PD. Married to Nic Dalton Montgomery, the owner and baker at Succulent Sweets. Parents to Abigail and Finn. {Tied With Me}

Caleb Montgomery – Navy SEAL. Married to Brynna Vincent Montgomery. Parents to Josie, Maddie and Michael. {Safe With Me}

Will Montgomery – Quarterback for the Seattle professional football team. Married to Meg McBride Montgomery, a nurse at Seattle Children's Hospital. Parents to Erin and Zoey. {Play With Me}

Julianne (Jules) Montgomery McKenna – Entrepreneur. Married to Nate McKenna, the co-owner of their joint business. Parents to Stella. {Fight With Me}

Dominic Salvatore – Illegitimate son of Steven Montgomery. Owns vineyard and winery. Married to event planner Alecia. Parents to Emma. {Forever With Me}

Ed and Sherri Montgomery – Ed is Steven Montgomery's brother. Parents to Amelia, Anastasia and Archer.

Archer Montgomery – Eldest of the siblings. Real estate mogul. Married to Elena Watkins. {You Belong With Me}

Amelia Montgomery Crawford – YouTube sensation, makeup brand owner. Married to Wyatt Crawford, architect. {Stay With Me}

Anastasia Montgomery O'Callaghan – Wedding cake designer and baker. Married to Kane O'Callaghan, world-renown glass blowing artist. {Dream With Me}

The Crawford Family

Melody and Linus Crawford – Parents of Wyatt, Levi and Jace.

Wyatt Crawford – (Mentioned above) – {Stay With Me}

Jace Crawford – Best cardiothoracic surgeon on the west coast. Married to veterinarian Joy Thompson Crawford. {Love With Me}

Levi Crawford – Detective for Seattle PD. Married to mega pop star, Starla. {Dance With Me}

The O'Callaghan Family

Tom and Fiona O'Callaghan – Parents of Kane, Keegan, Shawn, Maeve and Maggie.

Kane O'Callaghan – referenced above. {Dream With Me}

Keegan O'Callaghan – Owner of O'Callaghan's Pub. Married to Isabella O'Callaghan, meteorologist. {Escape With Me}

Shawn O'Callaghan – Screenwriter. Married to Lexi Perry, novelist. {Imagine With Me}

Maeve O'Callaghan – Real Estate Agent {Flirt With Me}

Margaret Mary O'Callaghan – Youngest sibling. Widowed.

The Martinelli and Watkins Family

Vinnie and Claudia Watkins – Deceased. Parents to Elena Watkins. Vinnie is the former boss of the mafia syndicate.

Carlo and Flavia Martinelli – Carlo is the current mob boss. Parents to Carmine, Shane and Rocco.

Elena Watkins – Referenced above. {You Belong With Me}

Carmine Martinelli – Eldest son. Mafioso. {Underboss}

Shane Martinelli – Middle son. Mafioso. {Headhunter}

Rocco Martinelli – Youngest son. Mafioso. {Off the Record}

Other Important People

Asher Smith – Former partner to Matt Montgomery. Now lives in New Orleans, married to Lila Bailey, a college professor. {Easy With You, a 1001 Dark Nights Novella}

Bailey Whitworth, Gray McDermitt, Kevin Welling – {Burn With Me}

Benjamin Demarco – Owner of Sound Fitness, a gym in downtown Seattle. Married to Sabrina Harrison. {Shine With Me, a 1001 Dark Nights Novella}

Noel Thompson – Interior decorator. Sister to Joy Thompson. Married to Reed Taylor, a financial advisor. Parents to Piper. {Wonder With Me, a 1001 Dark Nights Novella}

ABOUT THE AUTHOR

Kristen Proby has published more than fifty titles, many of which have hit the USA Today, New York Times and Wall Street Journal Bestsellers lists. She continues to self publish, best known for her With Me In Seattle and Boudreaux and Big Sky series.

Kristen and her husband, John, make their home in her hometown of Whitefish, Montana with their two cats and dog.

facebook.com/booksbykristenproby
instagram.com/kristenproby
bookbub.com/profile/kristen-proby
goodreads.com/kristenproby

NEWSLETTER SIGN UP

I hope you enjoyed reading this story as much as I enjoyed writing it! For upcoming book news, be sure to join my newsletter! I promise I will only send you news-filled mail, and none of the spam. You can sign up here:

https://mailchi.mp/kristenproby.com/newsletter-sign-up

Other Books by Kristen Proby

The With Me In Seattle Series

Come Away With Me
Under The Mistletoe With Me
Fight With Me
Play With Me
Rock With Me
Safe With Me
Tied With Me
Breathe With Me
Forever With Me
Stay With Me
Indulge With Me
Love With Me
Dance With Me

Dream With Me
You Belong With Me
Imagine With Me
Shine With Me

Check out the full series here: https://www.
kristenprobyauthor.com/with-me-in-seattle

The Big Sky Universe

Love Under the Big Sky
Loving Cara
Seducing Lauren
Falling for Jillian
Saving Grace

The Big Sky
Charming Hannah
Kissing Jenna
Waiting for Willa
Soaring With Fallon

Big Sky Royal
Enchanting Sebastian
Enticing Liam
Taunting Callum

Check out the full Big Sky universe here: https://
www.kristenprobyauthor.com/under-the-big-sky

Bayou Magic

Shadows
Spells

Coming in 2021: Serendipity

Check out the full series here: https://www.
kristenprobyauthor.com/bayou-magic

The Romancing Manhattan Series

All the Way
All it Takes
After All

Check out the full series here: https://www.
kristenprobyauthor.com/romancing-manhattan

The Boudreaux Series

Easy Love
Easy Charm
Easy Melody
Easy Kisses
Easy Magic
Easy Fortune
Easy Nights

Check out the full series here: https://www.
kristenprobyauthor.com/boudreaux

The Fusion Series

Listen to Me
Close to You
Blush for Me
The Beauty of Us
Savor You

Check out the full series here: https://www.
kristenprobyauthor.com/fusion

From 1001 Dark Nights

Easy With You
Easy For Keeps
No Reservations
Tempting Brooke
Wonder With Me
Shine With Me

Kristen Proby's Crossover Collection

Soaring with Fallon, A Big Sky Novel

Wicked Force: A Wicked Horse Vegas/Big Sky Novella
By Sawyer Bennett

All Stars Fall: A Seaside Pictures/Big Sky Novella
By Rachel Van Dyken

Hold On: A Play On/Big Sky Novella
By Samantha Young

Worth Fighting For: A Warrior Fight Club/Big Sky
Novella
By Laura Kaye

Crazy Imperfect Love: A Dirty Dicks/Big Sky Novella
By K.L. Grayson

Nothing Without You: A Forever Yours/Big Sky
Novella
By Monica Murphy

Check out the entire Crossover Collection here:
https://www.kristenprobyauthor.com/kristen-proby-
crossover-collection

Made in the USA
Monee, IL
16 August 2021

75786242R10162